"Guess what

His voice was

look into his eyes. It was a mistake, because she saw something there she hadn't seen before.

She saw desire.

Ridiculous, she told herself. "Stop playing games with me."

"Why?" he asked, then pulled something out of a bag. It was the book, *his* book. She wanted to strangle him.

"What makes you think I'm interested?" she asked.

"The love scene on page eighty-four, if nothing else," he said with a grin.

"Don't be absurd."

"Aren't you curious?" he asked.

"Not in the least," she said, hoping her face hid the fact that the book hidden under the cushion beside her was open to that very erotic scene. Against her will, she wondered what it would be like to forsake her reading and spend the night with the author? It was a shocking thought that didn't shock her.

"I spent all last night," Carlson said casually, "trying to decide if your garters were satin or lace. I should have known your tastes would run to satin—you're sleek, not frilly."

Her eyes widened and her head jolted downward until she was staring at her legs—and her garters—and her stockings. How had she let that happen? She grabbed the nearest cushion and covered her knees. Both their gazes locked on the book that had been hidden beneath the cushion—and the smile on Carlson's lips as he met her eyes told her he knew all her secrets. . . .

WHAT ARE *LOVESWEPT* ROMANCES?

They are stories of true romance and touching emotion. We believe those two very important ingredients are constants in our highly sensual and very believable stories in the *LOVESWEPT* line. Our goal is to give you, the reader, stories of consistently high quality that may sometimes make you laugh, sometimes make you cry, but are always fresh and creative and contain many delightful surprises within their pages.

Most romance fans read an enormous number of books. Those they truly love, they keep. Others may be traded with friends and soon forgotten. We hope that each *LOVESWEPT* romance will be a treasure—a "keeper." We will always try to publish

LOVE STORIES YOU'LL NEVER FORGET
BY AUTHORS YOU'LL ALWAYS REMEMBER

The Editors

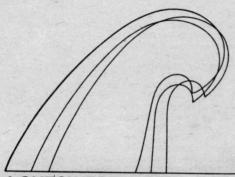

LOVESWEPT® • 490

Victoria Leigh

Little Secrets

 BANTAM BOOKS
NEW YORK • TORONTO • LONDON • SYDNEY • AUCKLAND

LITTLE SECRETS

A Bantam Book / August 1991

*If you would be interested in receiving protective vinyl
covers for your Loveswept books, please write to this address
for information:*

Loveswept
Bantam Books
P.O. Box 985
Hicksville, NY 11802

ISBN 0-553-44141-8

Published simultaneously in the United States and Canada

PRINTED IN THE UNITED STATES OF AMERICA

OPM   0 9 8 7 6 5 4 3 2 1

Little Secrets

One

Her breath caught in her throat as it always did when she saw him.

Cassandra Lockland watched through a narrow slit in the drapes as Carlson slid out of the midnight black Jaguar at the curb. Her gaze missed nothing of what he wore . . . or of how he moved. The light camel-colored blazer was cashmere, she knew, because she'd seen it before. The open-necked shirt would be crafted of the finest linen. He always wore the best. His slacks were dark brown, a light wool, she imagined. And his shoes were of a soft, polished leather that made no sound when he walked, a circumstance that had unnerved her more than once.

Her heart pounded in her ears as he looked up at her two-storied Victorian home, his slow, deliberate study of it terrifying. He seemed to stare right where she hid in a corner of the bay window in the living room, behind a camouflage of drapes and lacy flounces. Panic nearly sent her running, and she was certain he knew exactly where she was—and why.

In a moment, it was over. He turned away, leaving

her wondering if her imagination was riding some cosmic roller coaster. She stood transfixed, her breathing shallow as Carlson flexed his shoulders a couple of times. He could be tense from working all day on another book, but she knew better. He was tense about tonight.

A smile curved her lips as she tried to imagine how he felt about coming to a party in her house—a party in his honor. Friends of his had told her that for Carlson, parties were at best boring, at worst, extremely irritating. In that case, it wasn't surprising that he highly disapproved of what she did for a living.

He didn't particularly like her on a personal level, either, and that also did not surprise Cassandra. She *knew* she wasn't his type. But that didn't explain why he seemed to go out of his way to aggravate her. Her smile vanished as she remembered when he'd run into her at the supermarket a few weeks earlier, and had had the gall to ask if the frozen dinners in her basket were for that night's honored guests.

No, Cassandra didn't like Carlson either.

It was just that she felt so incredibly alive when he was near.

He'd be annoyed tonight, she knew. Annoyed yet resigned, because his closest friend, Mallory, had arranged the party before she'd told him, and there hadn't been a damn thing he could do to stop it.

As Cassandra watched, Carlson strode around to the driver's side of the Jaguar and helped Mallory out. She could hear their laughter, Mallory's feminine voice mixing with his rougher one. Cassandra had heard his laugh many times, usually right after a red flush had begun to creep up her face following one of his verbal assaults.

She should have hated that laugh.

She felt a pang of something akin to envy as

Carlson escorted Mallory up the first set of steps at the bottom of the walk, slipping an arm around her waist as she teetered on incredibly high heels. Cassandra could almost imagine the warmth of that arm, the security it offered, and wondered if he'd be as solicitous to her under similar circumstances.

She sincerely doubted it. Carlson generally managed to make her feel like a bug under a microscope, an amusing object for scrutiny and nothing more. Bugs weren't afforded courtesies of any sort.

She shivered away the imaginary warmth and concentrated instead on the man who was fast approaching her home. Autumn's early evening sun slanted through the trees, catching him full in the face and highlighting the smooth, clean lines of his jaw, the neatly trimmed mustache, the high cheekbones beneath his reflector sunglasses. Thick, dark brows rose above the aviator frames that hid his laugh lines and shielded his expression.

Her last view of the couple was as they mounted the steps to the porch. Carlson lifted his free hand and raked long fingers through his thick, sun-streaked brown hair. When his hand fell away, his hair looked as though he'd spent an hour getting it just so. It was as disciplined as the rest of him.

The door chime sounded, and she could hear one of her staff rushing to answer it. Taking a deep breath, Cassandra eased the drape back into place and prepared herself to meet Carlson head on. The tough part was over, she told herself. He couldn't take her by surprise.

That was why she'd been watching for him. Without the element of surprise, she could govern her reactions.

She realized it hadn't worked when she stopped herself an instant shy of wiping sweaty palms down the sides of her silk skirt. Grabbing a cocktail napkin from a nearby table, she blotted the evidence of her nerves. It was getting worse instead of better, she thought angrily, this attraction she felt toward a man she could barely tolerate.

Cassandra admitted her attraction to Carlson as readily as she worked to circumvent it. Except for the odd meeting at the market or gas station, avoiding him wasn't all that difficult nowadays. She'd met Carlson through Peggy Markham, her former housemate. Peggy owned and managed a flower shop just down the street from Mallory's art gallery, and she and Carlson had dated for several months before both decided it wasn't quite what they wanted. Even so, the erstwhile couple continued to maintain a friendship. Until Peggy—now engaged to another man—had moved out two weeks earlier, Carlson had occasionally shown up to take her to some event or another.

The last time was a month ago. He'd caught Cassandra unawares in the back garden, sneaking up on those soundless shoes and asking something about Peggy that she couldn't hear over the pounding of her heart. She'd stared at him—forever, it seemed—then stuttered a few words about where Peggy was, hoping that was what he'd asked.

She had feared he'd noticed the slight flush that accompanied the quickening of her heartbeat. His eyes had narrowed and he'd examined her face thoroughly as she stared up at him. He'd held her with his gaze, letting her see the amusement in his eyes as he evaluated the panic in hers.

Then he'd told her she must have been thinking of the day's parties and not paying attention to details, because she'd mascaraed one set of lashes and not the other. Or perhaps one set was naturally blond and the other brown. Either way, he hoped she'd forgive his lack of manners for pointing it out.

Cassandra had muttered under her breath that a

gentleman wouldn't have commented upon it, but she'd been relieved that that was all he'd noticed. He hadn't seen the excitement, the attraction she felt each and every time they met.

He hadn't seen the need.

Carlson was tucking his sunglasses into his jacket pocket when he saw Cassandra step out of the living room into the front hallway. She looked slightly flustered, which surprised him. Normally she didn't lose her composure until he drove her to it.

He had seen that shadow at the bay window, though, and he knew she'd been watching for him. Waiting. The thought provoked all sorts of interesting ideas.

"You're looking lovely tonight, Cassandra," he said before she could open her mouth. "Your shadow doesn't do you justice."

Cassandra felt the dreaded flush crawl up her neck and tried to pretend she hadn't heard a word he'd said. She stared into his mocking dark brown eyes and wondered if there was anything he didn't know.

"What shadow?" Mallory asked Carlson over her shoulder as she greeted Cassandra with a brief hug.

"Hello, Mallory. Carlson." Cassandra decided to ignore him for the time being and looped her arm through Mallory's to draw her into the living room. "I'm glad you came early. We can go over the arrangements before everyone comes if you like."

"Don't be silly," Mallory said. "I hired you so I wouldn't have to bother with it, not to mention that I'd rather slit my wrists than arrange a cocktail party for so many people. What did Carlson mean about the shadow?" Mallory tossed her long auburn hair back from her face and stared at the obviously ruffled woman beside her.

"I'm sure I don't know," Cassandra said evenly. "Perhaps as an ex-spy, he sees shadows behind every . . . tree."

"I was never a spy," Carlson said, suggesting with a hint of raised brows that there might be another person in the room more deserving of the title.

"But I thought you did some undercover work when you were in the Navy," Mallory said, her gaze flitting from Cassandra to Carlson and back again.

"Underwater, you mean," he clarified.

"Underhanded, most likely," Cassandra muttered, then bit her lip in reprisal for the careless words. What on earth had gotten into her? As often as Carlson had baited her in the past, she'd never succumbed to voicing any of the multitude of insults she'd fabricated in her mind.

"What did you say?" Carlson asked. He thought Cassandra had said "underhanded," but that couldn't possibly be right. She'd *never* said anything even remotely impolite. Cassandra Lockland was much too refined to let emotion get in the way of good manners. Polite when flustered, composed when embarrassed, she never once let go. She would mumble under her breath, stare daggers at him, or turn her back, all vague signs of annoyance. Irritation, not real temper. He doubted if she had one because she didn't ever fight back.

He had been wondering for weeks now how many buttons he'd have to push to accomplish that particular loss of control, or if it were even possible.

"Underpaid," she said quickly, then changed the subject. "I'm sure the financial benefits from your service days hardly measure up to what you're earning as an author. Speaking of which, congratulations on *The Seventh Kiss*. I've been told it's doing quite well."

Carlson was disappointed. He'd thought for sure

she'd intended something more interesting than that polite turn of phrase. Perhaps there was nothing beneath her composed facade besides more composure.

"Which still has nothing to do with shadows," Mallory complained. When neither Carlson nor Cassandra spoke up to fill her in, she mumbled something about going into the kitchen to see if she could steal a couple of canapés.

Cassandra's heartbeat accelerated. Being alone with Carlson wasn't what she'd planned—but then she shocked herself by wondering what it would be like to be *really* alone with him.

"I'm surprised you know the title," he said, leaning against the back of a low chair, his legs crossed at the ankle.

Cassandra rallied. "Mallory sent over a few copies to use as decoration on the buffet table. I think the covers go rather well next to the roses, don't you?" As she gestured to the table, she moved several feet away from him.

She didn't understand why she didn't feel any safer.

"Roses?" He looked over her shoulder to where a pair of large vases of red roses flanked several copies of *The Seventh Kiss*. "The cover is yellow with the title in plain block letters. How does that go with red roses?"

"For a romance, the cover is rather tame, I suppose," Cassandra said, refusing to agree that the roses were a little on the overwhelming side. "Tight budget?"

"Good taste," he countered. "And it's a love story, not a romance."

"A romantic adventure," Mallory said as she rejoined them, her palm cupping several shrimp hors d'oeuvres and a wedge of smoked Gouda.

Cassandra was getting ready to ask for the definition of a romance versus a love story—and what made Carlson think he knew anything about either—when the doorbell announced their first guests.

Carlson watched her go, wondering if he'd imagined the flash of mischief that had lit her eyes, but he knew he hadn't. Cassandra had definitely wanted to score a couple of points off him, a prospect that didn't intimidate him in the least.

He could take care of himself.

He smiled, suddenly realizing he was looking forward to the night's entertainment. Harassing Cassandra would take the edge off having to endure this damned party . . . and it was certainly better than sitting around his houseboat with only an aggravating siege of writer's block to keep him company.

Cassandra slipped away from a lively debate about the merits of New Mexico wine versus that of Colorado, leaving the two sides arguing growing season and soil and price without ever hearing whether or not anyone had sampled the wines in question. She snagged a canapé from a passing waiter and murmured a suggestion that he begin to offer coffee to the guests.

That was all there was to it, more or less. Once the party was in gear, Cassandra had little to do that required more than a quiet reminder or meaningful glance to cue the staff for the next stage. The men and women who worked for her were good at what they did and proud of it. In her home, they could serve sit-down dinners for groups of four to forty, cocktail parties for up to sixty, coffees, luncheons, and brunches. And they would do it with a flair that was Cassandra's trademark, an ease that belied the hours of preparation that went into each event. Every affair was carefully planned, elegantly served, and wonderfully comfortable.

She made a point of that, maintaining the feeling that she was entertaining friends, not clients. In a sense, that was exactly what she did. All of her business came from referrals, friends of friends who needed to hold a party or meal someplace that wasn't an impersonal restaurant, and needed someone to plan the event who required no guidance except for the basics of guest list and budget.

Cassandra had fallen into the business of entertaining quite by accident. It had been her duty as a wife to entertain frequently, and now that she was a widow, it was her job.

She let her gaze drift around the room, counting the number of guests as she slowly crossed the oriental carpet, heading toward the bay window where Mallory was sitting with her husband, Jake Gallegher. With his late arrival, there were thirty-nine people, and she'd conversed with each of them at one point or another over the last couple of hours.

All except Carlson. At first, it had been easy to be where he was not. Her job had been primarily at the door greeting guests, while Carlson had stayed within the growing circle of friends in the living room. Now, with all the guests there, avoiding Carlson took a little more skill. He seemed to be everywhere at once, the honored guest making the rounds, accepting the congratulations of those who had gathered to celebrate with him. Cassandra knew a few of them as friends, several as passing acquaintances, the others as faces from the small community. Peggy was there with her fiancé as was Vincent, the chef from The Mill Grill, Jake's restaurant.

The Seventh Kiss, Carlson's second book, had been released just a few days earlier, and it seemed to

Cassandra she was the only person in the room who hadn't read it.

Nor did she intend to.

Carlson watched as Cassandra paused near the edge of the carpet, enjoying her tranquil ignorance of his presence and anticipating the moment when she'd become aware of him. As his gaze drifted down across her shoulders, he admired the perfect foil of turquoise silk against her blond, almost white hair. He didn't like blondes, he reminded himself, then decided an aesthetic appreciation of the woman was allowable. Cassandra was, after all, undeniably beautiful.

She was short, about five feet three, he guessed, and that was another strike against her. He preferred his women taller. He loved to dance, and bending over Cassandra would have him in traction within a week. Not that there was the remotest possibility of dancing with her. She was too delicate, too fragile . . . too much like his ex-wife.

Still he couldn't take his eyes off her.

He admired her composure, even as he strove to disturb it. She was adept at maintaining that air of cool serenity—but she wasn't perfect. He knew he'd unsettled her the minute he'd walked in the door, and he was determined to do it again. He looked forward to seeing the faint flush that would color her cheeks, the way her fingers would tighten around her glass.

It was time.

"Aren't you getting tired of waiting?"

Cassandra felt a few nerves pop at Carlson's husky words, and she conceded that she'd subconsciously given him the opportunity to approach her. Another ten feet and she would have been safely at Mallory's side, but she'd dawdled at the fringes of the gathering, daring him to strike.

And he was right. She was tired of waiting, but not for the reason he thought. This night would be different, she'd decided just moments ago. She'd replayed their earlier conversation in her mind and had discovered a certain thrill at saying what she wanted—even if it had been under her breath.

From now on, she was going to fight back.

She turned and smiled politely before saying the first thing that popped into her mind. "Tired of waiting for you to leave?"

She'd changed the rules, Carlson thought, eyeing her speculatively. Or she'd thrown them away altogether. Never once had she said anything so blatantly ill-mannered—at least, not when she thought he'd hear her. His breath wedged in his throat as he stared into her sea-green eyes and saw the challenge they held. There was a flicker of something else there, too, and he could have sworn it was excitement.

He very much wanted to believe that it was. They would have something in common, then, because he found the prospect of this new Cassandra incredibly exciting.

Just to make sure her comment hadn't been a momentary aberration, he prodded her again. "I meant that you might be tired of wondering when I was going to say something that might irritate you."

"A mosquito is an irritation," she said smoothly. "You're merely an annoyance that I wish to avoid."

He smiled slowly, dredging his memory for incidents that were bound to set her on edge. Now that he'd broken through her reserve, he wanted to see how deep her emotions went. The cool, composed woman he'd tormented for the past few months was suddenly human, and he was intrigued . . . tantalized.

"Now what could I have done that would make you say that?" he asked with innocent surprise in his voice. "You're not still mad about the mascara, are you?"

"No."

"The time I noticed the spider in your hair?"

"It would have been kinder if you had told me directly, instead of waiting until you and Peggy were gone and then suggesting she call from the restaurant. The spider might have been poisonous."

"It wasn't," he said with a grin, "and as I wasn't sure of the etiquette, I elected to wait and discuss the matter with my date."

"Your consideration underwhelms me," Cassandra murmured, running nervous fingers across the chignon on top of her head. She was more than a little relieved to discover the hairpins were still neatly tucked into place. Were that not the case, Carlson would undoubtedly have felt duty-bound either to say her hair was coming apart at the seams, or to ask Mallory to do it before something inappropriate dropped into the hors d'oeuvres.

Whichever way he handled the situation, it would have been played to maximize her embarrassment. He couldn't just say that a hairpin was escaping. There was no sport in that. Cassandra frowned because her normally immaculate appearance was something she took for granted. It was unsettling that Carlson could make her feel so defensive.

"Then it must be something else I did that annoyed you," he said. He snapped his fingers as though a revelation had come to him. "Was it the flowers I sent to Peggy that you thought were for you? Although why you imagined I'd be sending you flowers has always made me a little curious."

"That was a long time ago," she parried, though she remembered the day with disconcerting clarity.

He shrugged. "I don't know how long you hold a grudge."

"My name was on the card," she said, biting off the words as the color rose in her face.

"Just the envelope," Carlson said genially. "The note inside was for Peggy. I didn't want the flowers to get lost and it made sense to put your name on it for the florist."

"Her name wasn't on it at all."

"An oversight on my part."

An oversight. Cassandra remembered how her heart had pounded after reading those words he'd meant for Peggy and not for her. *I look forward to an evening with you, alone.* Innocuous enough, but they had made her feel something she hadn't felt in a long time.

They had made her feel wanted. He called them an oversight.

"Sending flowers to a florist wasn't the most romantic gesture in the world," she said.

"Peggy was on a diet. I couldn't exactly send candy, now, could I?" When Cassandra didn't answer, he switched to another track. "Then I guess you're still mad about the night I mentioned you had a run in your pantyhose?" He nearly laughed aloud at the image of Cassandra twisting around and bending in embarrassingly awkward positions to check. He'd tricked her into looking. There hadn't been even a snag.

"They were stockings, not pantyhose!" she fumed, then gasped when she realized what she'd said.

"You looked, though," Carlson managed to say, though speaking was abruptly difficult. All he could think about was that she'd been wearing stockings, and that meant there'd been a garter belt and soft, creamy skin in between. His heart thudded in his chest as heat shot through him, and it took an incredible act of will to calm himself. Releasing carefully controlled breaths, he tried to mark it down to a simple generic response to any female, because he didn't have those kinds of reactions to Cassandra.

Still he couldn't help wondering if she was wearing stockings that night.

He was fascinated by the change in her. He'd thought of Cassandra as a challenge, an iceberg that he was interested in melting just to see if it could be done.

Tonight, he was seeing the fire beneath the ice. Tonight, he was discovering the woman.

Cassandra swallowed hard, watching a fierce hunger flash in his eyes. Maybe she should point him toward the buffet table before he keeled over.

Of course, there was more than one type of hunger, she thought, but she couldn't seriously imagine any of the alternatives applying to Carlson, not when he was talking with her, his favorite victim for his misguided sense of humor.

It was time, she decided, to give a little back. Glancing at the noisy crowd, she ensured that all was running smoothly before she took her first shot.

"Let's get back to our earlier discussion," she suggested with a sly smile. "You claim you write love stories."

"My publisher prefers to describe them as stories of adventure and intrigue nourished by a love alliance between the two main characters."

Her brows rose. "Adventure and intrigue?" She'd thought they were only romantic romps.

"Good guys and bad guys," he said, his eyes gleaming with amusement at her surprise. "But I still like to think of them as love stories."

"So what makes you an authority on love?"

Carlson was astonished by the boldness of her attack—and delighted to discover there was a breathing, thinking, *fuming* woman beneath that calm exterior. What on earth had gotten into her? he wondered.

"What makes you think I'm not?" he asked.

"Peggy mentioned a divorce in your past, which doesn't exactly support your batting average. And I haven't heard any gossip about your becoming embroiled in anything more than a casual affair."

"Love is a very personal thing. Perhaps I just don't advertise."

"Perhaps there's nothing to advertise."

Carlson had a hard time not laughing at that one. Cassandra was definitely getting in over her head.

"I think if you'll read the book," he said instead, "you might discover that I have a certain sensitivity with the two lovers. I tried hard to make their coming together a very real thing, not just a romantic fantasy."

So what's wrong with a little fantasy? a gremlin in Cassandra's mind shouted. She shushed the voice, because she'd rather sacrifice herself to a volcano than let Carlson know she'd indulged in some fantasy thinking where he was concerned.

"I guess I'll never know, then," she said, fearlessly meeting his gaze. "I have to admit that I only have time for . . . legitimate fiction."

He laughed. "Why, you little snob! What's not legitimate about adventure and intrigue?"

"You're the one who keeps saying you write romances," she retorted.

"Love stories," he corrected her automatically.

"Whatever. I'm just saying I don't read romances.'"

"*Dr. Zhivago* was a romance."

"And not in your league at all, I'm sure," she said, then wished she hadn't let herself be drawn into this losing battle. She'd been trying to prove to herself that there could never be anything but antagonism between them, that the attraction she felt was misplaced and best forgotten. So why did her hurtful words hurt her?

The silence between them stretched painfully long, then Carlson went on the offensive.

"I'm surprised you have time to read at all, what with all the parties you give around here."

"There's that," she said, relieved he seemed willing to change the subject. "They do seem to take up most of my time."

"Do you ever wonder what you'd do with your days if your friends didn't keep you busy, throwing all their entertaining problems into your lap?"

Cassandra gasped at the sudden panic that swept through her. Without so much as a by-your-leave, Carlson had plucked a very real fear from her most private thoughts and tossed it back at her as casually as he would swat a fly.

Without the business of entertaining, she'd have nothing.

She wanted to run, but her feet wouldn't move. She wanted to argue, but there was nothing to argue against.

She wanted to cry, but refused to give him the satisfaction. She'd hurt him with her uninformed censure of his career, and he'd reached out to hurt her back. Tit for tat.

They were even, but he'd landed the last punch.

Lifting her chin, she said she hoped he enjoyed the rest of the party, then turned to join a group that had gathered around the baby grand in the corner. Later, when the lights were out and the house was silent, she'd give in to the luxury of reliving everything they'd said and wonder why two relative strangers found it necessary to tear each other apart.

Cassandra ushered the last guest out the door and returned to the living room. Mallory was comfortably entrenched in the window seat. Jake and Vincent, who had come together, were hobnobbing with her cooking staff in the kitchen.

"Did I make a mistake in asking you to do this party?" Mallory asked when Cassandra joined her on the window seat.

Cassandra felt her lips curve, and was amazed that she was able to smile without forcing it. The last hour of the party had been the worst. As she'd worked her way through the guests, she'd known Carlson was watching her every move.

She couldn't figure out why.

He baited her, provoked her, went out of his way to tease her. Throughout the evening she'd been miserable and exhilarated and terrified all at once, but when he'd walked out the door with a woman friend who'd offered him a ride home, she'd felt as though something important was moving out of her reach.

"Of course you didn't make a mistake," she said to Mallory. "I'm the best person for the job, and I would have been disappointed if you hadn't asked me. I'm just not sure Carlson appreciated being stuck in my home for the duration. You know how much he disapproves of me and my parties."

"Carlson is the closest friend I have outside of my husband," Mallory said, "and he isn't doing anything or acting in any way that I recognize." She leaned back against the cushions of the window seat so that she could put her feet up on a low table. "Even Jake mentioned that he was looking a bit worse for wear by the end of the party."

"I think I'm supposed to feel badly about that," Cassandra said slowly, "but I can't help but believe there was no avoiding it." Particularly since she'd decided to fight back. Getting nervously to her feet, she crossed over to the buffet table and scooped up his books.

"You should keep a copy," Mallory suggested as

Cassandra handed them to her. "I'd bet Carlson would even autograph it for you."

"Thanks, but no. Just having it in the house would be reasonable grounds for nightmares," Cassandra said, faking a shudder.

Mallory nodded, carefully hiding her smile as she understood what she'd been too ignorant to see in the first place. Carlson and Cassandra . . . steel and ice. An interesting combination, she thought. Not precisely opposites, but incongruous nevertheless.

"At least now that Peggy has moved out of the house," Cassandra said as she sat down again, "Carlson doesn't have to worry about any more encounters."

"Not here anyway," Mallory said. "But what about Peggy's wedding next month, or the charity gala I'm hosting at the gallery? Carlson will be there, you know."

"As will a few hundred other people," Cassandra said evenly, slipping out of her pumps and tucking her feet beneath her.

Mallory was not to be denied. "And what about the grocery store, the post office . . . the sidewalk? Mill Valley is a very small town." It was one of several like communities in Marin County, a generally affluent and highly eclectic area that clung to the northern end of the Golden Gate Bridge, just across the bay from San Francisco.

"He lives in Sausalito," Cassandra said. That was still in Marin County, she knew, yet quite possibly another world away. If left to chance, she might never see him again.

"But he's always shopped here," Mallory said, "because my gallery is in Mill Valley. Even though he doesn't do much at the gallery anymore, he's kept up the old habits."

Cassandra wasn't really listening, though. She and Mallory didn't stand a chance of making sense out of where and what and why Carlson did what he did. That was something only he could explain and she would never have the chance to ask. Cassandra faced her friend and set aside a lifelong habit of discretion as she asked what she really wanted to know.

"Does Carlson dislike me because I resemble his ex-wife in some way, or is it because of what I do for a living?"

Mallory grinned and said the one thing guaranteed to confuse and comfort Cassandra. "Carlson doesn't dislike you at all. He just thinks he does."

Two

Cassandra marched out of the bookstore with the package tucked securely under her arm, ammunition for the next time she saw him.

It hadn't been so much a choice as a compulsion, she admitted with a self-conscious twinge. Her curiosity had gotten the better of her.

She was dying to find out if Carlson was as dynamic in prose as he was in person. Pausing just past the store's awning, she took a deep breath and attempted to remember where she'd left her car.

"I was trying to decide between sending flowers or calling when I saw you standing there."

She felt the shock of recognition all the way to her toes. That smooth, masculine voice did it to her every time, brought her alive with a pulsing excitement she'd never felt around any other man.

She wished he'd fall into an open sewer.

Slowly, cautiously, she lifted her gaze to the man who invaded her dreams, even as she damned him for doing so. It wasn't an easy situation, being attracted to someone who was forever putting her on the defensive about everything from her personal appearance to her livelihood. He wasn't quite smiling at her, although there might have been laughter in the eyes behind his dark glasses. She really couldn't tell, and she told herself she didn't want to know.

"Didn't you get enough last night?" she asked, somehow keeping the hurt she was feeling out of her voice.

"Enough what?"

"Satisfaction." She shifted away from the sun so that she didn't have to squint up at him. "I'd have thought all those taunts about my shortcomings would have satisfied you for more than a few measly hours."

"I'm sorry."

"Excuse me?"

"I said I was sorry. That's why I was debating about the flowers." Carlson nudged his sport coat back and pushed his hands into the pockets of his trousers. "I was afraid you'd take it badly, what with the last time I sent flowers to your place and all. But I figured you'd rather have something pretty than talk to me again, and I couldn't think of another way to apologize." He reached up to pull the glasses from his eyes, showing her that he wasn't laughing at all.

Cassandra felt like crawling under a rock. He had the decency to apologize when she hadn't given it a moment's consideration. She'd been too angry . . . and too sensitive to the truth of what he'd said.

"I wish you wouldn't," she said finally.

"Send flowers?"

She shook her head. "Apologize. Because if you do, then I'll owe you one and I'm not ready to do that yet."

"I don't expect you to change your opinion about what I write and why I do it," Carlson said quietly. Despite his words, though, he imagined the sun didn't shine as brightly as before. Why was her approval so damned important to him now, when he hadn't cared about it before?

Cassandra smiled a little. She had absolutely no intention of reversing her stand on his writing, not unless it was warranted, and she had little faith that the book under her arm would provide sufficient grounds for such a reversal. A Pasternak he was not.

He couldn't be.

"That's not what I was referring to when I said I wasn't ready to apologize," she said, self-consciously adjusting the package so there was no chance he could see the book within. "I won't apologize for my opinions. It was expressing them that was tactless."

"And you're not going to apologize for that either," he concluded.

"I don't think so." Unable to resist, she added, "But if I did apologize, it would probably be for being more sensitive about my work than you are about yours." She smiled again as she mentally patted herself on the back for phrasing that so nicely.

"It was never my intention to hurt you," he said seriously. "You took a couple of shots at my career. I thought it was open season." He shrugged. "I guess I took better aim than you."

Cassandra watched the play of emotions in his eyes and knew he spoke the truth. Relief washed over her in silent waves as she realized he really didn't know her deepest fears. It had been a coincidence, nothing more. He'd stumbled across a weakness without seeing it for what it really was. She'd been so terribly afraid when he'd said it. No parties, empty days, meaningless hours with nothing to keep her busy. A useless, unnecessary existence. In the stillness of the night, alone again in her home, she'd worried that he might know other things, other feelings she needed to hide, especially from him.

In that moment, Cassandra decided she was going

to be nice to him. He had apologized and she was left feeling incredibly ashamed of the way she'd behaved. She'd realized too late that fighting back didn't necessarily mean fighting dirty.

An apology was something she definitely needed to give him, she realized. And she wanted to do it today, before it was too late.

Too late for what? she asked herself.

"Will you tell me something, Cassandra?"

She'd forgotten for a moment that he was there, and his voice startled her. "What?"

"Will you tell me *why* what I said scared you . . . hurt you?" Carlson had spent most of the night thinking about it—a long night without even his writing to distract him, the writer's block firmly entrenched and growing more ominous with each hour. But he hadn't worried about that last night. His thoughts had been filled with Cassandra and the pain he had caused without meaning to.

He'd meant only to needle her about her party-filled schedule, yet she had stared back at him wordlessly, her expression filled with such hurt that he'd been incapable of reacting. Not that she'd given him a chance. She'd frozen up as though she'd never been warm in her life, politely wished him a pleasant evening, and run away before he'd had time to take in the sudden turn of events.

He'd intended to tease, not wound; mock her as she'd mocked him.

"No, I won't tell you," she answered him.

He wasn't surprised. Nor was he a quitter. He smiled to assure her he had no intention of hurting her as he had the night before. "No, never? Or no, not now?" he asked lightly. He could feel her relief, but he wasn't sure if it was because he was succeeding in lightening the mood or if she was grateful for something else he didn't understand.

Cassandra was just brimming with intriguing little secrets that he intended to uncover.

"No, not in your lifetime," she said distinctly, allowing a cautious smile to return. "Thank you for the apology, though."

"You're welcome." At least he no longer felt like a slug for what he'd said, although he was still confused over where she'd drawn the line between hurt and mere embarrassment . . . and why.

Standing there, alone with Carlson in the sunshine of a suddenly gorgeous day, Cassandra discovered that she didn't dislike him nearly as much as she had thought. After all, he couldn't be such a bad guy if he could apologize without knowing why. "You know something?" she asked.

"What?"

"You can really be a nice man once in a while."

"Nice?" He tried to sound outraged. "*Most* women find me charming."

"Kind of boggles the imagination, doesn't it?" She laughed as she turned to walk toward the northern parking lot, even though she hadn't the slightest confidence her car would be there. It didn't matter, because as long as she was moving, she wouldn't have to work so hard to hide what she was feeling. Carlson wouldn't be able to look into her eyes and discover how much she was drawn to this playful side of him.

Carlson fell into step beside her, her laughter a sensual rub that almost literally knocked him sideways. He realized he'd never heard her laugh like that before. It was a low, husky sound that made him want to hear more. He looked down at her, his gaze taking in the carefree sweep of hair that she'd fastened in a knot on the top of her head, a few loose curls swinging freely across her shoulders as she moved. Her hair glinted white gold in the sunshine, and looked as soft as a duckling's feathers. He wondered what it would feel like to touch, to loosen the knot and let the luxurious waves flow over his hands. One curl tempted him in particular. It was caught beneath the collar of her blouse, and he found himself tugging it free, his fingers brushing her neck in the process.

"What are you doing?" Cassandra squeaked, her voice an octave above any range she'd previously accepted as normal. But she couldn't help it, so surprised was she by his fleeting touch. She loved it, the wild current that shot through her body, but she batted at his hand because he wasn't supposed to touch and she was *not* supposed to like it.

"Something impulsive, Silk," he said smoothly, not quite meeting her eyes because touching her had done something to him that he hadn't expected. He rubbed his fingers together, remembering the slide of silk between them and wondering how soon it would be before he could do it again, before he discovered all her textures.

His heart was pounding with the realization that touching Cassandra had ignited needs and desires he'd never associated with her. Touching her had made him want her, and had made him admit it.

It wasn't altogether a sensible thing, wanting a woman who equated him with pond scum, and Carlson decided he'd been out in the sun too long.

Cassandra could only maintain her glower for a minute. *Silk*, he'd called her. She absorbed the word and shivered in the warmth of the early fall morning.

As she wondered what possible response she could make, the aroma of fresh coffee floated out from a nearby kiosk, assaulting her with the reminder that she hadn't had her first cup of the day.

She wondered what Carlson would say if she offered to buy him a cup and hoped it wouldn't be something like "Is this a date?" She swung out of the sparse flow of human traffic and turned to face him, skeptical that this was such a good idea. "I'm stopping for some coffee," she said. "Do you want some?"

"Is this a date?"

She groaned. "I *knew* you were going to say that!"

He laughed. "All right, how about this? Is this dutch or do we flip for it?" Carlson was suddenly having fun, and he suspected Cassandra wasn't as exasperated as she was acting.

As if to prove him wrong, she shot him a scowl, marched over to the kiosk, and ordered a single cup of coffee.

It was every man for herself.

Carlson drifted over behind her and ordered a cup of tea, then flipped a dollar and change onto the counter to pay for both.

Cassandra said "thank you" very properly and without any sense that she really meant it, then led the way to an umbrella-topped table. She was still annoyed about the date thing, not because he'd said it but because she knew him well enough to know he'd say it.

That was doubly infuriating, because she felt like she didn't know him at all—not this man who was dishing out apologies and smiles and gentle caresses.

Carlson slipped in front of her to hold her chair, an unnecessary gallantry given the circumstances, but one she decided she didn't mind at all. Particularly given her earlier assumption that he'd never behave in a chivalrous manner toward her. But when he pulled out the chair right next to her for himself, she wished she'd picked her own place, on the far side of the table. Surreptitiously, she slipped the book from under her arm and placed it beneath her purse on the chair on her other side.

"It was a nice party last night," Carlson said. He still didn't like the idea of Cassandra—or any woman, for that matter—depending upon the good graces of friends and acquaintances for anything. It was bad enough that she was partying away her life, but what really provoked his aversion was that she was using the parties to get by, clinging to a way of life she'd lost when she was widowed. If she could only break away, she might become a strong, independent woman.

Carlson was very attracted to strong, independent women. It was the fragile, dependent, clinging types he couldn't stand. Like his ex-wife. She'd been as clingy as they came.

"I'm glad you enjoyed it," Cassandra said smoothly, not quite looking at him. She didn't want to get back into how the evening had ended.

Apparently, Carlson was sensitive enough to figure that out. "I noticed you were in the bookstore," he said cheerfully, his gaze going to the chair where the book lay. "What's that you have there? Dostoyevsky?"

Cassandra winced. Tiny lightning strikes still danced on her spine from that moment when his fingers had brushed against her. It had been barely a touch, but so incredibly intoxicating that she'd gone out of her way to spend another few minutes with him. Now, however, he was distracting her with something even more devastating.

She blanched as she thought of the book, and wished fervently that she'd brought a larger purse so she could have shoved the stupid thing inside, away from his prying eyes. But she should have known she couldn't get anything past a former bodyguard/security expert/Navy Seal, and whatever else that went into making Carlson an extremely dangerous man.

"It's none of your business," she said primly, fussing with her purse to make sure the book was as well-covered as possible.

Carlson took one look at the flush that stained her cheeks, then deftly leaned over the table and snatched the package from the chair before Cassandra could react. He grinned as he slipped off the bag to reveal the yellow cover. "*The Seventh Kiss.* Not a bad choice," he said, effortlessly holding the book away from her grasping hands.

"It was the first thing I saw," she said, certain he wouldn't believe her.

He didn't. "Afraid I'll get a swelled head because you deign to pay good money for the sweat of my brow?"

"No." It was already swelled, she thought, hanging on to her determination to be nice.

"I'm willing to bet you'll love it," he said. "Especially page eighty-four. That's the first real erotic scene in the book." His grin became cocky. "I had you in mind when I wrote it."

Cassandra was seething inside, absolutely furious that not only had she bought the book, but he'd caught her! And how dare he taunt her with the *erotic* parts and try to attach inspiration to her! She knew what he thought of her, and it had nothing to do with sex.

This was worse than the time he'd found her singing along with Mr. Rogers on television, her delight in the children's program making her unaware of her audience until she'd heard his deep, rumbling laugh. She'd turned on him, scarlet with embarrassment, but hadn't been able to get a single word out. He'd backed out of the room, his mischievous eyes promising future reminders of the incident.

Cassandra dug her nails into her hands and reminded herself that she was supposed to be nice. She wished her fingernails were digging into *his* hands, though. But one look at his expression and she knew that was exactly what he wanted her to do—fight back, react to his outrageous kidding so that he could tease her some more.

She refused to do it.

"I'm sure you tell all the women of your acquaintance that they're your inspiration," she finally said. She plastered a sweet smile on her face so he'd know he wasn't getting to her. It was a futile attempt at deception, though, because she could feel the heat of a deep red flush throbbing in her cheeks.

His grin deepened in proportion to her agitation. "I hear that the critics are calling this a break-the-rules book that unites the sensual delight of a romantic awakening with a convincingly realistic plot of intrigue and adventure, a romance made believable within a cloak of terror."

"I thought you said it was a love story."

"It is, but some people don't seem to know the difference between that and romance and I've not bothered to argue the semantics."

"And *you* know the difference?" She couldn't help it. The note of incredulity was blatantly there, as "nice" got overwhelmed by the need to wipe that smug expression off his face.

His grin eased into a lazy, sensual smile. "Of course."

"Tell me." She was finding it a little hard to breathe, what with the way he was looking at her and the seductive curve of his lips daring her to say things she'd never said before.

"I'd rather show you," he drawled, leaning back in his chair.

"Don't be ridiculous," she said weakly.

"I'm not," he murmured, and offered her the book back.

Cassandra just shook her head, frightened of the sensual force that seemed to come from within her, but, in truth, was radiating from the man sitting next to her. It was too dangerous, getting this close. She knew he didn't like her, yet she felt a frightening compulsion to tell him how much she wanted that to change.

She sprang to her feet, ignoring his protests because she had to get away. She even took a few steps before realizing her purse was on the chair and she couldn't leave without it.

"You don't have to run," he said, handing her the purse and trying to give her the book at the same time.

"I'm not running," she said, and foolishly looked into his eyes. He didn't believe her, and that made her even more determined to try to hide what was obviously a mad dash for sanity. "I'm late for an appointment. Thank you for the coffee."

She left the book in his hands, knowing that right then, having it with her was as much a threat as being with the man who wrote it. She faked a smile and walked quickly down the mall and into the parking lot. She loitered there for about ten minutes, fuming as she paced up and down the aisles. She'd belatedly remembered that her car was on the other end, and she absolutely refused to renegotiate the mall until she was sure he'd left.

When she finally ventured back to the shops, she moved furtively, watching the shadows for her nemesis to reappear. At the bookstore she bought another copy of *The Seventh Kiss*. Now more than ever she needed to learn something about the man who tied her in knots without seeming to try.

She wondered if he even knew what he was doing to her.

• • •

Cassandra waited until the bath was full before shrugging off the soft peach silk wrapper and stepping into the lavender-scented water. It was just the right temperature—a couple of degrees shy of boiling—and she sighed in contentment as she submerged herself up to her shoulders.

The healing force of the steaming water began to work its miracles as she slowly relaxed, her body unbelievably tense from the afternoon's tiny calamities. It hadn't been the smoothest of days, what with the wine merchant delivering the wrong case—she'd chosen Pinot Blanc, not Pinot Noir—and then the puff pastry shells from the bakery had been all wrong, cupcake-sized molds and not the miniature ones she'd ordered. They'd had to make do with the shells, trimming and cutting until the finished product resembled canapés more than sandwiches. But she'd sent the wine back in a jiffy, telephoning the manager of the shop in the meantime to ensure the correct case would arrive in plenty of time for chilling.

Then the gardener's lawn mower had shot a pebble into a front window. She'd had to organize that repair quickly, because a cracked window made the house look a bit tacky, and that wasn't exactly the image she wanted to portray.

And through it all, she'd suffered the distinctly uncomfortable notion that she'd never be able to put Carlson very far from her most intimate thoughts.

She wanted him, needed him. It was no longer mere attraction, but a desire to be with him as a woman needs to be with a man. And that, she told herself firmly, was as much as she was willing to admit.

Cassandra sighed heavily and reached for the hand

towel she'd left on the tiled ledge beside the tub. Carefully, she patted her hands dry—or as dry as they could get, with all the steam still rising from the bathwater.

In her mind, she ran over the final preparations for the cocktail party, knowing her small staff would have everything under control when she returned downstairs later. She'd allowed herself an hour's respite from the subdued bustle of the kitchen, an hour to soak away the tensions of the day before slipping into the black wool sheath she'd chosen for that evening.

An hour in which to begin *The Seventh Kiss*.

Checking the clock that stood on the vanity across the tiled floor, she decided she'd procrastinated long enough and picked up Carlson's book. With fingers that were shaking ever so slightly—she blamed the debilitating effects of the near-scalding water—she opened it to page one.

She was determined to read it cover to cover, but no longer was it ammunition she was seeking.

It was understanding.

Three

Cassandra tried very hard not to slam the door. It was terribly difficult, though, because it seemed as if she'd been waiting for hours for everyone to leave.

The party's over! she'd felt like shouting at least an hour ago, when the host-client had suggested everyone gather around the piano for a rousing round of fifties favorites. Hardly anyone could remember much of them, but they'd tried anyway.

Moving back to the living room to help collect glasses, dishes, and other residue, Cassandra could only think that if she was very, very lucky, the remaining staff would soon leave her in peace to finish *The Seventh Kiss.*

She could hardly stand the anticipation.

Sonia, her second-in-command, had practically had to drag her out of the bath just hours ago. She'd been so engrossed in the book, she'd ignored both the clock and her conscience. She'd had to hurry, then, twisting her hair into something that more or less resembled her usual neat, dignified chignon while Sonia fussed about how late it was getting and didn't she always greet her guests at the door?

Cassandra had, but only barely. And with more than a thread of impatience, which she would have questioned if she'd had the time.

Or the nerve. She liked what she'd read of *The Seventh Kiss*. She liked it a lot.

All she cared about now was reading more. This was going to be, she knew without a shred of doubt, an all-nighter.

Before that, though, there was the tidying up that was always necessary after any party. It was a chore that night—which it had never been before—and it took almost forever. Finally it was done and Cassandra ushered her helpers out the door with an eagerness she hoped didn't show, but she knew it did.

She poured a glass of wine—her first for the evening, because a slightly off balance hostess was unacceptable in her book—and kicked off her shoes, then curled up in the cushioned seat of the bay window with *The Seventh Kiss* and her own anticipation of what was to come.

She knew she wouldn't be disappointed.

It was more than a romance . . . although that might have been enough, the way he did it. *The Seventh Kiss* was a love story from the very beginning. It was sensual and fun and exciting, and she wondered if his first book was as good as his second.

It was more than a romance . . . an adventure within a web of intrigue that sucked her out of the real world, transporting her to a place that was more real, more alive than anything she'd ever encountered.

It was more than a romance . . . and whatever doubts or uncertainties she'd harbored with respect to Carlson's creative talents were vanquished.

He was better than good.

Cassandra opened the book to where she'd left off, not needing to review the last few pages. There wasn't the slightest chance she'd forgotten a single word. Instantly she was enthralled with the book she'd fought against buying, then paid for twice.

Alex and Katherine were not mere characters of fiction. They were real, their story vividly alive. Cassandra lived it with them, brushing away suffocating cobwebs with Katherine's grim acceptance of unavoidable unpleasantness, and trying not to cringe as the heroine squelched through the murky waters of the drainage ditch.

Alex was hard and uncompromising, totally in control until the terror struck and sent the two of them running. Even then, Cassandra could feel his confidence, and it reassured her as it did Katherine. Alex's arrogance was restricted to the facts of who he was and the things he knew, a compelling trait that drew Katherine to him even as she fought her dependence upon him.

She accepted his desire for her as it was offered: A temporary thing, a convenience . . . a ploy that would bind her to him when she would have struck out on her own. The fact that he used it cold-bloodedly frightened her, but beneath his indifference was a fire even he couldn't control.

It was that fire that gave Katherine the strength to be with him.

A soft knock sounded at the front door. It frightened Cassandra for a moment, because unexpected arrivals weren't good news for Alex and Katherine. The interruption was even more unwelcome than usual, considering Alex was currently engaged in a determined effort to erase the ordeals of the day from Katherine's mind, employing a sensual assault that was at once calculatingly erotic and wonderfully tender.

The knock came again, at last, startling Cassandra out of Carlson's make-believe world.

Taking a moment to calm her racing heart, she wondered what guest had returned to find a lighter or glasses or missing earring. But then she looked at the grandmother clock on the wall and realized few people would have the nerve to call this deep into the evening. It was after eleven.

She wedged an opening in the lacy curtains and peeked outside. A familiar dark blue Mercedes sedan was parked beneath the streetlight out front.

Carlson.

She nearly panicked, her breath catching in her throat as she reviewed her options. She could ignore him, pretend she'd already retired for the night.

But the living room lights were still on. He'd know she was hiding. She rejected that plan as indefensible. She didn't want him to think she was a coward . . . no matter how cowardly she felt.

On the other hand, she could go to the door and see what he wanted. That was where the cowardice came in, though. Facing Carlson wasn't something she wanted to do.

She felt too weakened by his written words to hide what she was feeling inside, too much involved with the story he'd created to distinguish between the man and the book, the reality and the fantasy.

It didn't help that the incredibly erotic love scene between Alex and Katherine had confused her sensibilities and confounded her senses. It aroused in her feelings that had lain dormant for so long, she barely recognized them. Feelings she couldn't deny . . . and didn't want to admit to anyone. She found it hard enough admitting them to herself.

There was a third knock, a shade louder. With a deep intake of breath that was meant to give courage and strength and just plain sustenance, Cassandra tucked the book under a cushion and walked to the door.

Her pulse soared and her face flushed with heat as she opened the door, but there wasn't anything she could do about it. Carlson stood motionless in the wash of light from the hallway, his eyes narrowed against the glare, his brows drawn into a forbidding scowl.

"You shouldn't open the door at this time of night," he said sternly, "without checking first to see who's there."

It peeved her that he assumed she had the brains of an infant, and contrarily she didn't correct him. "If I'd known it was you, I wouldn't have opened it at all." Holding her ground just across the threshold of her home, she toyed with the crystal doorknob and tried not to squirm under his hard stare. She waited in silence as his gaze raked her from the top of her head to her stocking-covered toes.

"That's not the point," he growled. "A woman alone shouldn't take chances like that."

"Did you come all the way from Sausalito just to give me your 'woman alone' lecture or is there something else you want to annoy me about?"

His scowl deepened. "I didn't come over here to annoy you."

"Amazing what you can do without even trying, isn't it?" she said easily, surprised at how adept she'd become at this game. Perhaps it was her only way to salvage anything from this mess—like her pride.

Aggravating a man was certainly a lesser offense to one's dignity than revealing one's attraction to or, heaven forbid, amorous interest in, that same man. Especially when he was only interested in her as a specimen for study, and an amusing one at that.

Amorous interest! Cassandra almost fell over when she realized what she'd thought. Of all the irrational things to pop up at inopportune moments. Amorous interest indeed.

She'd be a fool to imagine her feelings for Carlson were anything more than a minor attraction. Moderate attraction, she corrected herself as she composed her expression and looked blankly at him.

"Invite me in, Cassandra," he said quietly.

"Why?"

"I'll tell you inside."

"It's late," she whispered, wishing he'd say something that would give her an excuse to slam the door in his face.

"I know. I wouldn't have stopped at all if I hadn't seen your light."

He would have cruised past and she wouldn't have known it. Cassandra wasn't sure she wouldn't have been better off.

"I won't stay long," he said, and smiled.

It was that determined smile that swayed her. She stepped back and held her breath as he brushed past her, the soft suede of his sport coat a fleeting caress on her bare arm. She shivered and knew she'd made a mistake.

She should have never opened the door in the first place, and now it was too late.

Her fantasy had just walked into her home.

He paused beside her, waiting until she'd closed the door. "Your lights were on," he said, as though he needed to explain why he'd stopped, "and I could see your shadow in the window."

"I might have company."

"But you don't." He grinned, and she felt short and at a definite disadvantage as he looked down at her from a height emphasized by her bare feet.

"What makes you so sure I'm alone?" she asked, annoyed at his assumption, even if it was the truth.

"Because if you weren't, I would have seen two shadows at the window." Still, his gaze scanned the empty living room and hallway before coming back to her.

"There are other rooms in this house," she said stubbornly. Still, she was relieved he hadn't assumed anything at all. His information had been gleaned by way of deduction, not prior knowledge of her habits.

He shook his head slowly, negating her attempt at subterfuge. "You're alone."

"How do you know I'm not expecting someone later?" she asked recklessly.

That wiped the grin from his mouth. "Are you?"

Her pulse raced as she realized it mattered to him. "No," she said.

A gently chiding expression darkened his eyes. She tensed when he lifted a hand to her face, his thumb stroking a line from chin to ear as he spoke softly. "Don't tease about those things, Silk."

His touch was light and warm and slightly rough, and she had to concentrate hard not to shut her eyes and lean into it. "What things?" she breathed, wanting him to define the rules. She was definitely at a loss as to what game he was playing tonight.

He only shook his head, smiling slightly as he dropped his hand.

"You called me Silk," she said without moving.

"Yes."

"Why?"

His smile deepened, and he led the way into the living room, saying that as long as he was inside, he didn't intend to stand in the hallway. She followed, his broad back a great deal less threatening than the peculiar glint in his eyes that made her feel undressed, even though all she was lacking was her shoes. Silk, he'd called her for the second time that day. And he'd touched her as though he enjoyed doing it.

Stuff and nonsense, she scoffed, knowing it was

The Seventh Kiss that had sent her imagination reeling. A bug under a microscope, she reminded herself. That was how he regarded her and it was sheer idiocy to pretend otherwise.

Carlson was her adversary, not her lover.

He ignored the sofa nearest the door, the trio of love seats that were grouped near the tip of the piano, and the pair of wing-backed Queen Anne chairs facing the fireplace. Instead, he deliberately crossed to where she'd been seated earlier, then turned and waited for her to join him. She hesitated before reaching the cozy semicircle of chairs, wondering if she was supposed to offer him a drink.

"I wouldn't mind a taste of that wine," he said.

Mind reader, she grumbled silently. Heading over to the sideboard that served as the bar, she collected the open bottle of Pinot Blanc and another glass. After schooling her expression to one of polite composure, she returned to the bay window. Carlson relieved her of the bottle and delicate crystal goblet, then leaned down to add a measure of the wine to her glass before pouring his own. She reclaimed her previous spot on the window seat, and he settled into an overstuffed armchair close by, throwing out his long legs and crossing them at the ankle.

Cassandra sipped her wine in silence, waiting for Carlson to tell her why he'd come. She hadn't a clue. Silk, he'd said, and that didn't make any sense either. It almost sounded like an endearment, and that was the last thing she'd ever expected to hear from his lips.

A streak of stubbornness kept her from asking, though. Carlson would tell her when he was ready, if he decided to tell her at all. That much she did know about the man.

So why was he there? she wondered, and her heart

thudded in her chest as an absurd fantasy about herself and Carlson flitted across her thoughts.

Cassandra, she lectured herself firmly, you're a lunatic. Carlson has as much interest in you as you *ought* to have in him. That is, nill, nada, negative.

What a futile imagination she'd been stuck with.

She sat stiffly erect and watched as he lazily sipped from his glass of wine, which seemed so much more fragile in his big hands. Perversely—because she normally worked hard to ensure her guests' comfort—she begrudged his relaxed posture. She was totally incapable of imitating it herself. Without her high-heeled pumps, her toes barely touched the floor. There was nothing she could do about that except put on her shoes, and that wasn't an option. She didn't want to call attention to her stocking-covered feet. The last time he'd looked at them, she'd felt almost naked.

She took another gulp of wine and wished he'd tell her why he'd come before she made a fool of herself. It was so easy to do, given the company she was in.

"Stop fidgeting," he said abruptly.

"I'm not fidgeting." She squirmed a little to try to get comfortable, then leaned forward to place her glass on the coffee table. She nearly lost her balance because her toes weren't quite on the floor.

"You're making me nervous," he muttered, and stared hard at her until she quit moving altogether, her body locked in anxious rigidity and a ridiculously uncomfortable position. It seemed to satisfy him, though, because his next words were less harsh. "I brought you something."

"What?"

"Guess."

His voice was seductively low, enticing her to look into his eyes. It was a mistake because she saw something there she hadn't seen before.

She saw desire.

That was ridiculous, she told herself. "I can't guess. And as it's getting close to the witching hour, I'd advise you to quit playing games."

"Why?"

Her lips tightened mutinously as she decided she'd stop letting him bait her. Silence could be his answer.

He grinned, apparently reading her mind again. She watched in bewilderment as he leaned forward and reached one hand around to the small of his back. The hand returned with an object which he tossed onto her lap.

It was yellow. It was rectangular. It was a book.

It was *the* book.

She wanted to strangle him.

He was there because of that damned book. She'd been a fool to think he would have come for any other reason and was determined never to let him know she'd imagine anything else. She lifted her brows and cast a curious, indifferent look in his direction. It was no small effort. "What makes you think I'm interested?"

"Page eighty-four, if nothing else," he said with a grin.

"Don't be absurd."

"But this is just the copy you bought today," he coaxed. "I'm only returning your property."

"Impulse buying should be outlawed," she said sweetly.

"Aren't you even curious?"

"Not in the least." The book under the pillow beside her was open and obviously in the process of being read, and she'd burn in hell before she admitted it to him.

"Then I guess I wasted a trip," he said, his gaze

following the twitching movement of her hands as she plumped a pillow.

"Sorry about that." Cassandra hated herself then. Her feigned attitude wasn't even gratifying, considering how much she liked his work and how little effort it would take to tell him about it.

Over her dead body.

She quit fighting discomfort and swung her legs up, tucking her feet under her bottom. Breathing a sigh of relief, she leaned back against the cushions. Her nerves were calming, which surprised her. Carlson was still in her house, and that fact alone should have made her apprehensive. But she wasn't. Not much anyway.

She wondered when he would leave, now that he'd returned the book, and tried to convince herself that she wanted him gone so that she could get back to devouring *The Seventh Kiss*. But what would it be like to forsake the reading and spend the night with the author?

It was a shocking thought that didn't shock her.

"I spent all of last night," he said idly, "trying to decide if your garters were satin or lace. I should have known your tastes would run to satin. You're sleek, not frilly."

Her eyes widened and her head jolted downward ninety degrees until she was staring at her legs—and her garters—and her stockings. Oh good Lord, how had she done that? She grabbed the nearest cushion and plopped it over her knees, her breath coming harsh and fast as she prayed a large hole would open beneath her.

Both their gazes locked on the book that had been hidden beneath the cushion. Carlson's book. Open to page eighty-seven.

Carlson grinned. He was amused. And beguiled, aware that Cassandra was more nervous than ever and he was the cause of it. There was a different kind of tension in her than before, he realized. Different because she was aware of him as a man and not merely as an antagonist.

Different because she understood that awareness and was fighting it with everything she had.

He was charmed.

"Katherine wore stockings," he said, his voice low and full of a sensual awareness that penetrated Cassandra's bristling defenses and touched her in places he had no right to be.

She gritted her teeth audibly. "Lots of women do."

"Alex thought she'd done it just for him."

"He's mistaken," she retorted.

Carlson laughed. "Either way, it excites him."

Cassandra squirmed, wishing she had something to throw at him that would knock him out long enough for her to escape. She considered the pillow on her lap, but knew the fluffy attack would only amuse him and she'd be left with exposed garters again.

"Does it excite you?" he asked.

"What?"

"Page eight-four, eighty-five, eighty-six . . ."

She tried hard to say no. Her lips formed the word, but the noise didn't follow. She fell silent.

Carlson tried another angle. "Katherine wants to be loved."

"She's a fool." It was an artificial situation, Cassandra told herself, danger and intrigue shadowing real life. Katherine wouldn't find love there.

"For wanting love?"

"For expecting it from that man."

"You don't think he feels something for her?" Carlson picked up the book and flipped back a couple of pages, then began to read when Cassandra didn't answer. "*His arms curved around her shoulders, holding her gently, firmly. He didn't want her to flee. He wouldn't let her. He needed her too badly, just as much as she needed him.*

"*He wanted to drive the terrors from her mind because the dreadful fears he saw in her eyes tore him apart. He wanted to give her comfort. He wanted to fill her dreams with something that wouldn't haunt her in the darkness of the night.*

"*A little enough thing, but he wanted to give her a part of himself.*

"'*I can't—*'" *she began.*

"'*We can.*'

"*Alex was determined to insist, but he knew he wouldn't have to. He'd have to be blind not to know she wanted him.*"

"Stop it!" Cassandra felt the color leave her face, then rush back four shades deeper, a hot red that she could feel with the hands she slapped to her cheeks.

Carlson grinned wolfishly and continued reading.

"'*I'm not prepared . . .*' *she protested.*

"'*I am.*'

"'*It's been a long—*'

"'*Hush.*'

"*He finished the word at her breast, his mouth tugging at the hardened nipple that was still encased in layers of clothing. Katherine moaned as if his lips were hot and wet on her naked skin.*"

"I can't believe you're doing this!" Cassandra exclaimed.

"You don't like it?" Carlson asked, and his eyes dared her to touch that line with a ten-foot pole.

Cassandra didn't even think it.

"Give me a break, Carlson," she begged. "I'm a very shy woman."

"You can be shy and like it at the same time."

She tried for logic. "I thought you hated having your work read out of context."

"I've never tried it before," he admitted, his mustache twitching as he valiantly controlled his laughter. "But I have to admit it feels kind of kinky. Besides, I was trying to prove a point."

"Point taken," she said hurriedly.

"You agree, then, that Alex cares for Katherine in more than a sexual way."

"Agreed." And she envied Katherine for that. It had been a long time since her husband Michael had died, five years since she'd put aside those yearnings to love and be loved. She hadn't thought of herself as pining away for a man who was dead, but not once since Michael's death had she felt the need to be with another man.

Not until she'd met Carlson. Now she felt the sensual tightening of her body, a response as much to the words he'd written as to the man himself. The erotic scene captured her imagination . . . and made her want to feel what Katherine felt, to yield to Carlson's caresses as surely as Katherine yielded to Alex.

"Do you think they'll find love?" Carlson asked softly, all amusement gone. Cassandra was flushed, but not angry. He noticed that she wasn't looking at him but through him, her gaze focused on a distant image he could only speculate on. Her lips were slightly parted, and he noted her shallow breaths as the pink tip of her tongue slipped out to moisten those lips.

And against the soft wool of her dress, he could see the hard thrust of her nipples.

A taste, he told himself. He needed to taste her lips, touch her, so that he could prove it wasn't his imagination that was responsible for the arousal he saw in her. Then he'd leave, before things got out of hand. Cassandra wasn't the type of woman to be rushed. She needed to be courted.

He intended to begin tomorrow, and was wondering if a single night's courting would be enough to win her over. He was suddenly quite impatient to become intimate with the lovely Cassandra soon. A temporary intimacy, of course. They were too different to expect to share anything more.

For tonight, though, he wanted a taste. His mouth watered in anticipation.

She still hadn't answered him. Slowly, so as not to startle her, he put the book aside, rose from his chair, then slid onto the window seat. Not touching, not yet, he asked again, "Do you think they'll find love, Cassandra?"

She was aware that he was there . . . and why. It was like her fantasy come to life, and she was almost afraid to breathe, afraid the illusion might disappear in a puff of smoke. Katherine wouldn't have been afraid, she thought. Nervous, perhaps, but not afraid. And Cassandra knew that Carlson wouldn't do anything to hurt her. Embarrass her, perhaps, but never hurt.

She decided she could handle whatever embarrassment might come along. She might never get another chance.

"Silk?"

The low, beguiling voice reached her. "Yes?"

"Look at me."

"I am."

He shook his head. "You're seeing Alex, not me. I'm not Alex, you're not Katherine." Carlson wasn't about to look back on this time with Cassandra and wonder if she'd been aroused by the fiction he'd created. He wanted her aroused by him. "It's me. Carlson."

She blinked, and he could have sworn she was exasperated by his insistence. "I know that."

"Good." Remembering her shadow at the window, he reached past her shoulder to flick off the reading light. He wanted whatever happened between them to stay just that—between them. In the soft darkness of the room, with the light that spilled in from the hallway at a comfortable distance, his gaze found hers—wide-eyed, slightly nervous, but definitely determined.

She was going through with this—whatever it was—whether she liked it or not, he realized, and had to try very hard not to laugh. She'd been married once and yet she was acting as though this was her first intimate encounter.

He liked that idea.

"I'm going to touch you now," he said.

Good, Cassandra thought, and smiled at her impatience.

Four

Carlson bowed his head and put his mouth to where her dress hugged a burgeoning nipple.

Cassandra's eyes widened even farther and her hands flew to his shoulders, shock vying with arousal as she tried to decide whether to push or pull.

She'd just begun to draw him more firmly to her breast when he retreated a few inches. She felt incredibly let down. The heat of his mouth had been intoxicating, exciting, and she wanted more.

"I just had to try it," he murmured, his gaze taking in her disappointed expression as his lips moved toward her mouth. "Alex always has such terrific ideas. I'll do it again. Later," he promised, and captured her open mouth under his.

There was no slow introduction to his kiss. He claimed her lips with his and his tongue demanded she surrender everything . . . and more.

Cassandra complied because there was nothing else she could do. She'd been kissed before, but never had she felt so much a part of it. Within milliseconds she was an equal partner in the adventure. Her tongue rasped alongside his, then retreated to tickle the mustache that sensitized her lips and made her wonder how it would feel at her neck, her breasts, her thighs.

Carlson laughed into her mouth, then delved deeper. Her response was magnificent; nothing like the stoic widow he'd taunted over the past months.

Cassandra was exciting . . . and thoroughly excited, he thought with a sense of wonder. She hid so much passion beneath her reserve. His mouth slid up her cheek to close her eyes. It was disconcerting to have her gaze follow his every move. She was so avid and curious and totally involved.

Watching had its own place, but for now he wanted her only to feel.

Her lips released his name when his mouth covered her ear and his tongue caressed and teased. Then he felt as though the breath had been punched out of him as she twisted away and attacked him in turn. She wasn't at all reserved, not now, not with his encouraging whispers that seemed to inspire her to respond, and to assert her own demands.

He slipped a hand under her knees, straightening her out to lie beneath him as he pressed her back into the cushions, his mouth hovering over hers with murmured threats of retreat if she didn't comply.

Cassandra surrendered without a second thought, her mouth seeking his but settling for the suede cloth of his jacket when it was all she could find.

She wanted more.

His lips touched her temple, then returned to her breast where her dress clung wetly. He'd promised her he'd do it again. This time his teeth lightly grazed the hard nub . . . and he knew she liked it because her body arched into his with a strength that nearly landed them both on the floor.

Sanity returned to him from out of nowhere. *The Seventh Kiss*, he remembered.

He took heaving breaths as he rested his chin on her forehead, his fingers tangling in the satin garters at her thighs, just itching for the go-ahead.

He couldn't give it.

Body parts fought his decision. He ached everywhere, particularly where his hips cuddled Cassandra's. His mouth wanted to discover the softness of her breast beneath her dress. His fingers danced impatiently in that tantalizing never-never land between her stockings and panties.

Her pebble-hard nipples thrust grievously against his chest, and he would have given his life for the chance to feel her naked against him.

But it was Cassandra he wanted, not Katherine. And without Alex.

For the first time in his writing career, Carlson regretted the sensual prose he'd written. He shifted a little, enough so that he could talk.

"I want you." It was the most honest thing he could say.

Cassandra blindly sought his mouth and was disappointed when he evaded her. It was disconcerting, to say the least.

Perhaps he was telling her that kisses were not enough.

Perhaps he was waiting for the words.

"I want you too," she whispered. The admission extinguished any remnants of reserve that lingered within her. She'd never said that to anyone, not even her husband. He'd preferred to make love in silence.

Her words nearly upset Carlson's resolve, as a craving he'd never known before swept through him. He nearly gave into it. But he didn't, since he lacked the insight to ascertain if he'd led her to this admission . . . or if it had been Alex.

It was a sobering thought.

"I'll remember you said that," he promised huskily,

dropping a kiss on her cheek. "And if you forget, I'll be there to remind you."

Carefully, gently, he lifted himself from her. Braced on his arms, he looked for a long moment at her thighs where satin garters, silk stockings, and creamy skin made the most erotic picture he'd ever imagined. Unable to stand it any longer, he sat up, snatched a pillow from the many on the bench, and plopped it onto her lap.

So much for temptation.

I'll be there to remind you. His words echoed in Cassandra's mind. Did that mean he intended to tease her about her total loss of control? Bastard! she thought, then admitted that, bastard or not, she wanted him to touch her again.

She tried to focus on him, but he seemed just beyond her reach, the man who'd driven her crazy for months with his taunts. Now he had something new to tease her about.

And that was the up side. Knowing he might never touch her again was a devastating blow.

"That was certainly an interesting moment to change your mind," she said. She hoped he wouldn't notice the catch in her voice. Play it light, she told herself. Pretend it had been an experiment. *Nothing better to do with my time,* she imagined herself saying. *It was pleasant, but I've got to organize the pantry now. Good night, Carlson.*

Carlson saw the hurt in her wide, accusing stare. And the anger. He couldn't blame her. He didn't feel so hot himself. Moving with less ease than usual because his body wasn't exactly willing to forgive the punishing reversal of intent, he returned to his chair.

"I guess I was counting on you to slap my face or something before things got out of hand," he said.

"And miss my chance to neck with a famous

author?" Cassandra forced a smile and sat up, careful to keep the pillow on her lap because she wasn't up for discussing garters and the like.

Carlson leveled a hard look at her and slowly shook his head. "Don't say things like that, Cass. I don't like it." He leaned forward to pick up his wineglass, halting the impulse to return to where he'd been—half-lying on top of Cassandra with his mouth and hands all over her—and remind her of how hot and exciting it had been for both of them. He took a small sip, then returned the glass to the table. "We're not going to sling insults at each other anymore," he said softly.

"But I thought saying things like that was all part of the game."

"Tonight wasn't a game. I told you I wanted you. I meant it."

"No, you didn't." They wouldn't be sitting there talking if he did, she thought, because she wouldn't have done a thing to stop him.

He sighed. "Oh, Silk, you make things so damn hard." Sinking down into the overstuffed chair, he clasped his hands behind his head and leaned back to stare at the ceiling. That way he wouldn't have to look at her.

She was too tempting a picture by far, her hair all mussed and the imprint of his mouth still visible on her dress.

"Will it make sense if I tell you I just don't want you *tonight*?" he asked.

She didn't say anything and he didn't blame her. He could have put it better.

He tried again. "That was a misstatement of the facts. I do want you tonight, but I'm not going to do anything about it."

"I can't believe we're having this conversation," she

said, half laughing because the whole thing was becoming ludicrous.

"What happened a few minutes ago deserves a little talking about." Carlson was pleased to hear the lightness in her tone. He didn't want her to be angry.

He didn't want her to be hurt.

"It was an accident?" she offered brightly.

"No accident," he murmured.

"How can you want me that way if you don't even like me?" Cassandra was startled to hear herself say the words aloud, but it was so easy to talk this way, without his eyes boring into her soul and absconding with her truths, when she would have kept them hidden behind a facade of pride.

"Of course I like you."

"No, you don't."

"Whatever gave you that idea?" He liked her a lot more than he wanted to, he thought with a dry amusement.

"You mostly," she said.

"You mean because I tease you a lot?"

"That's putting it mildly. I sometimes feel like you're just waiting for me to do something stupid, and then I go ahead and do it because I can't seem to avoid it." He was still staring at the ceiling, and Cassandra took the opportunity to get comfortable again, tucking her feet under her thighs and taking care to keep the pillow in place.

"You're always so nervous around me," he said slowly, "I guess I started teasing you because I didn't understand why."

"And now you do?"

"I think so."

She waited with her heart in her throat, certain he was going to tell her that he'd known she'd been attracted to him all along. And that would be humiliating, the lonely widow making a fool of herself—

"I think I've been attracted to you all along," he said quietly. "That's probably what's been making you nervous."

The relief was all-encompassing. She felt it from her fingertips to her toes. But she knew he was talking through his hat.

"That's absurd," she said. "Peggy told me you have a thing about short blondes."

"A 'thing'?"

There was amusement in his voice and she liked it. When she felt one corner of her mouth lift in a half-smile, she realized she was enjoying herself. It was a little hard to believe, though, because just five minutes ago she'd been ready and willing to strangle him.

And just ten minutes ago she'd been ready and willing to make love with him.

"Not a 'thing' as in *like*," she clarified. "A 'thing' as in *dislike*. A pet hate, I suppose. Peggy didn't explain why." Actually, she had, but Cassandra wanted to hear it straight from Carlson.

"It's something to do with my ex-wife," he said vaguely.

"And that was . . . ?" she prompted.

"A lousy marriage. Nothing to do with you."

"Then you're saying you're attracted to me even though you don't like me." It was the darkness, Cassandra guessed. She wouldn't have had the nerve to quiz him on how he felt about her in the light of day. She was much too shy for that.

"I like you," he said gruffly. "It's not your fault you're a little on the short side. And blond."

"Thank you, I think."

Silence fell between them, emphasizing the darkness of the night, the clock against the wall ticking away the seconds and minutes. Cassandra didn't mind it, though. Sharing the quiet with Carlson was surprisingly companionable. Rocking forward on her knees, she retrieved her glass of wine from the coffee table and contemplated the amazing change of atmosphere between them. The clock struck the midnight hour, and she wondered how long he intended to stay.

"Have we settled the part about my not liking you?"

His gentle words roused her from her musings just enough to earn a response. "More or less," she said, "but I can't help pointing out that you can be attracted to a person without liking them." A case in point, she thought, was the way she'd felt about Carlson before his book showed her a new side of him.

But even that had changed, because she was beginning to like him very much. "You don't have to rationalize that you like me just because you're attracted to me."

He chuckled. "I don't think that's the situation here."

"What am I, then? The exception that proves the rule?"

"If you like," he said pleasantly.

"More likely a temporary deviation," she said flippantly. "You'll get over it."

Carlson's head snapped up. He didn't like the sound of that at all, which was confusing because she'd simply expressed what he'd been thinking himself.

"And in the meantime," he asked, "what do you suppose I ought to do about it, this attraction I'm feeling toward you?"

"Ignore it?" As if she could, she thought, knowing what she knew now—that the taste of him was more intoxicating than anything she'd ever imagined.

"Is that what you want me to do, Cassandra?

Ignore how I feel about you?" Did she really think it would be that easy? he wondered.

"Those aren't feelings. They're hormones."

"If it was all hormones, Silk, I wouldn't have stopped."

The bluntness of his response brought her to a full halt. She took a deep breath and raised her eyes to meet his. "So why did you?"

Slowly, each movement a conscious thought, Carlson leaned forward until his forearms were resting on his thighs. He stared at her for a long moment, reviewing what she'd said over the past few minutes . . . and thinking about the things she hadn't said.

When he'd been kissing her, touching her, she hadn't asked him to stop. And now here she was, bold as brass, asking why he had. Cassandra wasn't shy at all, he realized. She just thought she was.

Carlson decided he wanted to let her in on the secret.

"I didn't stop making love to you because it was the easy thing to do," he said, his gaze demanding that she not look away. "I did it because I need to know that you know the difference between me and Alex."

Cassandra was so delighted, she didn't bother to fake indifference. That was the last thing she felt, especially since it occurred to her that he was actually telling her the truth and there was a chance that someday he'd take up where he'd left off!

She smiled broadly. "Who's Alex?"

Carlson grinned. "Whatever gave you the idea you're shy?"

"I am!"

He shook his head. "Not even a little."

Perplexed by his denial of what she felt was a basic truth, Cassandra stared at him. And what did being shy or not have to do with the price of cake anyway?

"Tell me about yourself," Carlson said, wondering

how many other little secrets she'd hidden from herself.

"Why?"

He shrugged. "Because I'm a naturally curious person, I suppose."

She didn't believe him for a second. "What do you want to know?"

"Everything." Carlson was just beginning to realize that he knew very little about Cassandra at all. He was going to change that.

"It's late," she murmured.

"Tomorrow, then." Rising to his feet, he closed the distance between them and leaned down to drop a kiss on her forehead. It was all he would allow himself. "And I'll want to know then how you like the book."

"I can tell you now," she said, wanting the chance to take back all the mean things she'd ever said about his writing.

He shook his head and backed away a couple of steps, then turned to wind his way through the assortment of chairs and sofas. Reaching the archway that led into the front hall, he paused. "Tomorrow is soon enough. Come to Napa with me?"

Napa Valley, the most familiar of the wine areas in California, was just forty miles or so northeast of Mill Valley. It was liberally populated with new and old wineries, and was a fascinating place to visit. The autumn months were especially unique, with the crushing in progress.

"I haven't been there in years," she said wistfully.

"Then say you'll come," he coaxed.

"I can't." It about killed her to say it, because there was nothing else she'd rather do than spend the day with Carlson touring the romantic vineyards. Her fists bit into the pillow on her lap. "I've got a luncheon here tomorrow, then dinner in the evening."

"Sunday, then."

She shook her head regretfully. "Another dinner."

"Monday?"

"Yes."

"Yes, you have another dinner?"

"No. I meant yes, I'd very much like to go to Napa."

"With me?" He made it sound like a throwaway question—not really important, just asking—but he wanted to hear her say it.

"With you."

His fully approving expression rewarded her, and she couldn't help asking for confirmation of her own. "Why did you ask me?"

"To go to Napa?"

"No. Why do you want to be with me at all?" she asked quietly. "I need to know." She gazed at him fixedly, waiting for him to say it aloud so that there were no illusions.

"I think you do know," he murmured. "I told you before. I want you."

"That's all?"

"I want to have an affair with you, Silk." Carlson hadn't meant to say that, but she'd pushed, and honesty was one thing he would give her. A promise of forever wasn't.

His voice was a husky rasp on Cassandra's nerves and she wondered if she was making the biggest mistake of her life. Nonetheless, she was going to do exactly what she wanted and to hell with the consequences.

"I've never had an affair."

He nodded once, and expanded on the theme, as much to remind himself as to make it totally plain to her. "I like to believe that neither of us is stupid enough to believe we're building toward something permanent between us. But there's no reason we can't . . . enjoy each other for a while."

"We're unsuited," she said.

"Yes. But that doesn't have to have anything to do with what's happening now." Because that sounded so cold and it wasn't how he felt at all, he added, "I like you and care about you. I don't want you to get hurt."

"I won't get hurt."

He heard the conviction in her voice and wondered why he wasn't relieved.

"It's settled, then," he said. "Napa, on Monday. I'll call you this weekend to let you know what time." He said an abrupt good night and reminded her to lock the door after he left.

"Carlson?"

Her voice caught him just as he opened the door. "Yes?"

"I love your book."

Four hours later, Carlson was staring hard at the computer screen. Slowly, reading each word and stopping to make minor changes, he scrolled through the pages until he reached the end of what he'd produced that night.

It was good.

Heaving a sigh of relief, he saved the file and flipped off the machine. Book three was finally underway, and he had no fears that the crippling writer's block would return anytime soon.

He'd found inspiration.

Chuckling at how Cassandra would throw a royal fit if she knew his new heroine had inherited some of her more sensual traits, Carlson pushed away from the desk and headed into his bedroom. The long, wide window across from his bed faced the bay and he'd left those curtains open, closing others that looked out onto the next houseboat. Privacy, not darkness, was the motivating factor.

Dawn was hiding just over the horizon, although it was impossible to tell for sure. Fog had settled in sometime during the night and now blanketed the landscape of Sausalito. All he could see from his window was a kind of gray-white soup that seemed to cut him off from the real world.

It was time to go to bed.

Throwing his clothes onto a chair in the corner of his room, Carlson mentally reviewed the pages he'd written that night. Chapter one was well underway. And there was a love scene he'd completed that would fit nicely into a later chapter.

He smiled and said a silent thank you to Cassandra. Pulling up the heavy quilt, Carlson slipped between the sheets and shut his eyes.

He didn't know why he'd suddenly been able to write. He'd only realized on the short drive from Cassandra's that it was time to begin. And because it seemed like the logical thing to do at the time, he'd written a love scene. It was out of context, but that wouldn't make any difference. He could insert it where it belonged later.

It had been incredibly easy to write, not like creating fiction at all. He'd simply retold the fantasy of holding Cassandra and the excitement he'd found with her. It had made him want her all over again, the needs she aroused amplified by his repetition of the events. That had been the tough part, but he hadn't let it slow him down. The words had poured onto the screen, and when he was done, he'd put that scene aside and started with chapter one, page one.

Cassandra was a marvelous inspiration, yet she wasn't anything like his new heroine.

There was no physical resemblance between the two women: Melinda—the heroine—was a tall brunette. They had nothing in common on a professional level: Melinda was a highly respected art auctioneer.

Their personal lives weren't even similar. Melinda had divorced two husbands and was thinking about taking on a third out of sheer boredom when the hero stormed into her life and turned her world upside down.

Melinda was worldly-wise, independent, and thick-skinned. Nothing at all like Cassandra. And because of that, Carlson knew it would never occur to Cassandra to look for the most intimate of resemblances between herself and the heroine of his book. It would stay his secret.

Melinda's kisses were fiery. Just like Cassandra's. And that was only the beginning.

Cassandra would be outraged by what he was doing. He didn't intend for her to ever find out.

Five

He was back in stride.

A few hours' sleep, chores like eating and such that couldn't be ignored, then back to work. Carlson breezed through the first chapters of his new book with the confidence of a well-disciplined author.

Mallory called to ask him over for Sunday dinner and he begged off, then turned on the telephone answering machine. When the writing was going this well, he didn't like being distracted.

He made the necessary reservations for Monday and left a message for Cassandra, purposely calling at a time when someone besides her might answer. If he heard her voice, he'd be tempted to take a break and pop over for a visit. He wasn't supposed to spare the time, though, and while he knew she had a whole crew of people to help with the parties, he figured she needed to keep an eye on things.

He opened the second chapter with a violent scene that was part imagination, part memory of another life. After he'd sweated his way through the worst of it, he decided to write a short love scene to balance his mood, because he knew he wouldn't sleep with the violence uppermost in his mind.

He thought about Cassandra and about how much he was looking forward to seeing her again. With one corner of his mouth edging up in a smile, he opened a new file and created a sensual episode that stole his sleep in quite another fashion.

It took Cassandra two more nights to finish *The Seventh Kiss,* and she sacrificed a good portion of her customary nine hours of sleep because her days were packed with the weekend's scheduled events.

Every time she caught herself thinking about Carlson and the way he'd kissed her and how much she'd loved it, she redirected her mental processes toward something practical—like how many wineglasses needed to be organized for the bar, or whether paper cocktail napkins should be substituted for the cloth ones next to the shrimp sauce.

An affair, he'd offered. She was excited and nervous and wondered why there was a hard knot in her stomach each time she said the words. An affair.

Carlson called on Sunday and left a message with one of the cooks that he'd pick her up at five on Monday, if that was all right.

It was very all right with her, although she did wonder why they were going to leave so late. The wineries closed their tasting rooms in the late afternoon, usually four or four-thirty, and by the time they got into the valley, the sun would be setting.

Perhaps they were just going to dinner, she mused, and skipping the tourist bit. She decided to wear the emerald silk dress she'd bought the previous week. And she'd leave her hair down.

Carlson might imagine she'd been carried away by the story of Alex and Katherine Friday night, but she intended to set him straight. She wanted Carlson, the man, not the hero he'd created. And because that wanting was so strong and so difficult to rationalize in light of his wanting no more than a passing affair with her, she refused to think about it.

She'd have plenty of time for thinking when it was over.

Saturday's luncheon and dinner went off without a hitch, but Sunday's was turned topsy-turvy with the arrival of nearly twice the number of guests she'd been told to expect. Her elegant sit-down dinner for fourteen—the number of people her dining table could hold—became slightly less formal with the addition of three card tables scattered around the living room. While Cassandra led the guests into the glassed-in solarium at the back of the house for a final predinner cocktail, her helpers swiftly pulled out extra linens and place settings, and added candles and flowers to make the satellite tables as attractive as the larger one.

That was the easy part. Stretching dinner sent the kitchen help into a frenzy of improvisation. Black bean soup, spinach salad, pork tenderloin in raspberry sauce, and a rolled chocolate soufflé cake were reapportioned and supplemented with anything and everything that came to hand.

The client raved about the food, apologized for the mix-up in numbers, and gave Cassandra a hefty bonus for the inconvenience.

Cassandra sent out for pizza to feed the crew because nothing remained in the kitchen that even resembled leftovers.

Sonia stayed late to help polish the silverware, which a new waiter had dumped into the salad bowl in the rush of changing courses. Unfortunately, the bowl had still contained a mixture of vinegar and oil, and the forks had soaked there nicely until someone had discovered the blackened silver.

Sunday night Cassandra finished *The Seventh Kiss* and made plans to drop by the bookstore first thing in the morning to buy Carlson's first novel.

She had nothing better to do until five o'clock.

Cassandra pulled on the emerald silk dress over her stockings, satin garters, and lacy panties and bra. Turning to look in the mirror, she wondered how she'd managed the nerve to buy the sexy garment in the first place.

The bodice was simple and discreet, with a rounded neckline, cap sleeves, and a smooth fit. It was the drape of fabric across her hips that drew a person's eye to that part of her body, and changed the respectable, sheathlike dress into something faintly sensual. The long, loose-fitting jacket she'd bought to go with the dress did minimize the effect. It would do, she decided as she slipped on the jacket, then fastened a simple gold chain with a jade pendant around her neck. Fluffing her hair about her shoulders in a way that was quite the opposite of her typically sedate hairstyle, she wondered if she looked younger or just different.

She certainly felt different.

Grinning at her reflection, she pushed back the sleeves of the jacket to just below her elbows, then bent down to pull a pair of taupe suede heels out of their box. The shoes were new, too, purchased especially for the dress, a present to herself on that day last week when her accountant had declared her business was now making a consistently healthy profit. Until then, it had been more or less at the break-even point. That wasn't bad, except that she'd had to rely on the money left to her by her husband to pay all expenses that were not business-related.

She was entirely self-supporting now, the accountant had said. Her late husband's money could stay where it was, earning interest and giving her a fatter nest egg than she'd ever need.

Cassandra took that to mean she could buy a pair of shoes and feel no guilt. So she'd bought the matching bag too.

Snagging the purse from where it hung beside the mirror, she left her bedroom and headed down the curving staircase. She had a couple of minutes to spare and could read another page or two of *Applause of Angels*, Carlson's first book.

A knock at the door canceled that idea.

With a smile on her face that showed absolutely no reservations at welcoming the man she'd recently defined as an annoyance, she opened the door.

It was Carlson, as expected, looking absolutely fabulous in black slacks, a cream-colored linen jacket over a slightly darker shirt, and a silk tie of maroon and black splotches that should have looked awful but didn't. Cassandra was fully aware that he knew she approved because he smiled and said, "Thank you. I think you look pretty stunning too."

Actually, she looked like a million bucks, Carlson thought, and he wondered why she didn't leave her hair down more often. It was incredibly sexy like that, kind of mussed and looking as though her lover had been enjoying the feel of it.

"What's that?" she asked, looking over his shoulder toward the stretch limousine at the curb.

"A limousine," he said, ducking inside to snag her keys from where they lay on a marble-topped table. He urged her out onto the front porch and took care of the locking up as she stared down the walk at the white car.

"Trying to impress me?" she asked with a half-giggle.

"Are you impressed?"

"A little," she admitted. The hot excitement that flashed through her came as much from his hand at her elbow as from the idea of sitting with him, alone, in the back seat of that very large car. "Michael never used a limo unless it was an extra special event. Like a formal ball or something fancy like that."

The chauffeur was waiting with the door open, and Cassandra hid her chuckles as she ducked inside. Carlson followed her and the door clicked shut.

"This is a special event," he said. "We've never been on a date before."

"You're forgetting coffee the other day," she reminded him, grinning as she dropped her purse onto the seat beside her.

Carlson laughed and knew it was going to be a wonderful evening. "To be honest, I hired the car because it's no fun going to Napa if you can't enjoy the wines."

"You hired a limousine so you wouldn't have to drink and drive?"

"Mm. It seemed the thing to do at the time."

Cassandra settled back into the plushly upholstered seat as the car slid into motion, the chauffeur out of sight and out of mind behind a privacy screen.

They were alone—except for an open bottle of champagne in a wine cooler.

Carlson reached for the bottle and poured the best of Napa Valley's sparkling wine into two tulip-shaped glasses. Handing one to Cassandra, he made the first toast of the evening. "To inspiration."

"Inspiration?" She puzzled over it for a moment, then remembered him teasing her about page eighty-four of *The Seventh Kiss.* She shot him a look of patent disbelief and tasted the champagne.

Carlson just waggled his eyebrows and tipped his glass to his lips, his gaze holding hers over the rims of their glasses.

The car ate up the miles toward Napa Valley as they relaxed in the back seat and laughed over the champagne. It was such innocent fun that Cassandra found herself wondering if the word "affair" had actually been said aloud. They were acting like friends, not soon-to-be lovers.

Perhaps he had changed his mind.

"We're going on the Wine Train?"

"I thought you'd like it," Carlson said. He confirmed their return time with the chauffeur before joining Cassandra where she stood practically gawking at the departure station. He put his hand under her elbow and propelled her toward the steps. "When you said you hadn't been to Napa for a few years, I thought you'd get a kick out of seeing it this way. The train's only been operating for a year or so."

"It's an absolutely marvelous idea!" she said enthusiastically, then proceeded to swamp him with a deluge of questions. "How long is it? Where does it go? Do we get to stop at any of the wineries? Where are we going to have dinner? Will the car meet us at the other end?" She kept up the barrage until they were inside the station.

Carlson pulled her out of the stream of arriving passengers and answered her questions with an indulgent smile. "It takes about three hours in all, traveling from Napa and up the valley through Yountville, Oakville, and Rutherford. It stops at St. Helena and turns around. We end up back where we started. No, we won't be stopping at the wineries, but we'll have plenty of opportunity to sample local wines on board. And dinner is served aboard. I booked our table for the return seating."

"Wow."

" 'Wow'?"

She recovered her expected composure. "I meant," she said with a mischievous smile, "that it sounds like a lovely evening."

"I think I preferred 'wow,'" he said. "It goes better with the new hairstyle."

"You like it?"

"I'll let you know later," he said in a low voice, and stared long and hard at her before taking her hand and tugging her toward the ticket window.

For the first time that evening, Cassandra saw more than friendly amusement in his expression. She saw desire . . . and briefly felt relief before she was flooded with pangs of nervous excitement.

Carlson led her up to the window and confirmed their reservations. The train had just begun boarding passengers, they were told. Down that hallway, to the left. Have a nice trip.

They went with the flow, waiting their turn to have their photograph snapped by a liveried train employee. Carlson expressed amazed disbelief, then amusement when he discovered that Cassandra was camera-shy. He refused to allow her to skip it, though.

"I'll keep it if you don't want it," he said.

"Is that how you remember your lovers—a rogue's gallery?" she teased, then slapped her fingers to her mouth as she realized what an incredibly suggestive thing she'd just said.

Carlson grinned. "You're getting a little ahead of yourself, Silk," was all he said as he turned her to face the camera.

Cassandra was totally oblivious to the photographer as she tried valiantly to get her thumping heart under control. She was only partially successful by the time Carlson nudged her aside so that another couple could take their place.

They were guided to their car—an elegantly comfortable lounge with low seats and a few upholstered benches and tables—and offered comfortable armchairs that swiveled so that you could watch the passing scenery. It was stately and grand, and Cassandra forgot her temporary discomfort as she wondered if this was something like the Orient Express. She'd always wanted to take that famous ride from London to Venice, or even Istanbul, although it no longer went that far.

Carlson requested seats on the side facing east, then explained to Cassandra that the sun would soon be going down and until that happened, everyone facing west would be squinting into the sunset.

He'd done that the first time he'd come on the Wine Train.

"When was that?" she asked, swiveling her chair around to face him.

"Last year, about this time," he said. "I brought some friends from Pittsburg to see the valley. We spent a couple of nights in a bed and breakfast, visited a bunch of the wineries, ate at a couple of really great restaurants."

"And did the Wine Train."

He nodded. "It's great fun, especially if you like the relaxed approach to dining. There's not much to do except eat and drink, look at the scenery. And talk."

And talk. Remembering the other night when he'd asked her to tell him about herself, Cassandra guessed he meant to press her on it tonight. She wished she could make up something wildly exciting so that he wouldn't lose interest.

But then she realized that it wouldn't matter one way or the other. Interested or not, he didn't intend to stick around for the long haul.

They simply weren't suited.

An affair, she reminded herself. By definition, a

terminal relationship. She decided she wasn't going to waste a single moment of it wishing for more.

It could never be.

The train began its slow journey as Carlson picked up the drinks menu. They were debating the various wines when the waiter came by to make suggestions. They ordered a highly recommended special and were soon sipping a delightfully smooth and dry white wine from etched crystal glasses.

Cassandra stared out at the back streets and alleys of the town of Napa and wondered if the flutter of excitement in her stomach would respond better to a stiff Scotch.

"The scenery gets better," Carlson said dryly as they passed the back lot of some sort of construction or equipment rental company. "Once we get out of Napa, we quit peeking into backyards and the like."

"One does wonder what the residents think of the train," she murmured.

"As it's the only train to use these tracks, it seems to be unpopular in a few quarters," he admitted, and pointed to a sign that had "Wine Train" printed in a red circle with a line drawn through it. "There's quite a lobby against it. Besides tying up traffic for a few minutes several times a day, the wineries complain that it's taking business away from them because it doesn't stop."

"I'd think that tourists would do the Wine Train in addition to touring the wineries, not instead of."

"And keep a few cars of the already crowded roads," Carlson added. "Residents still complain that the added attraction of the Wine Train brings even more tourists to an already saturated area."

They sat quietly as the train wound its way through the suburban sprawl—back streets and road crossings and occasional glimpses of the old Napa, with some of its Victorian mansions restored to their original splendor, others looking the worse for wear. Cassandra remembered reading somewhere that the citizens of Napa had only recently begun to put a stop to the "progress" that had nearly destroyed their once fine city. "No growth" was the slogan, and it was no wonder that any increase in tourism would be regarded as counterproductive.

The train couldn't have been moving more than twenty miles an hour, she guessed, and was delighted when backyards and concrete lots gave way to vineyards. The autumn sun cast its rays upon row after row of vines, and if she looked closely, she could see which of them had already been harvested. Carlson pointed out that just because she could see grapes on the vine at the end of the row, it didn't mean there would be any fruit on the vines behind it. The harvesters sometimes left the last vine alone, a visual treat for tourists, he said practically. The romantic part of her made her wonder aloud if there was more to it than that. Superstition, perhaps. A gift to the gods.

Carlson raised his eyebrows and didn't disagree with her, which made Cassandra remember the romance of his writing . . . and wonder what it would be like to share her life with a man who could see the romance and live with the reality.

Safe, she thought. And deliriously happy.

Forget it, she told herself. Enjoy the moment.

As the Wine Train chugged its way up the Napa Valley, Cassandra wondered if she would have enjoyed living in the days when travel by train was the custom, not the exception.

"Have you ever ridden the Orient Express?" she asked Carlson.

"Just once. It was only a day trip in England. I didn't go across the channel and continue on through Europe."

"Was it wonderful?"

He nodded. "Brilliant, as the English would say."

"They say that?"

"A friend told me the younger crowd say 'brill,' but I never quite got the hang of that."

She laughed, trying to imagine Carlson saying "brill" with a straight face.

The waiter came by then with small plates of paté and cheese, which they placed on the sill beneath the windows. Carlson watched Cassandra nibble at her paté and wondered about the pansy on top. Was it edible, and, if it was, did he care?

He decided to wait and see what Cassandra did about the yellow and purple flower on her plate.

"Tell me about the Orient Express," she said around a mouthful of cheese. "I've always wanted to try it."

Carlson grinned and reached forward to flick a crumb from the corner of her mouth. His finger hesitated there for a moment, and he thought about how soft her lips had been under his, full and wet and tasting of excitement. He remembered her soft moans and wanted to hear them again, but he satisfied himself with dragging his finger across her full bottom lip before retreating.

"The Orient Express," he said easily, despite the wild beating of his heart. Cassandra's eyes were wide and expectant, and he knew she wasn't thinking about trains at all. "It was a terrific experience. The trip was about seven hours long. The train stopped at Leeds Castle, then wound its way through southern England before returning to London."

Carlson rested an elbow on the arm of his chair, shifting closer so he could talk without raising his voice. He tried to keep his mind on what he was saying, but her perfume invaded his senses as he spoke, a scent of lavender and springtime, and he knew he'd never smell lavender again without thinking of her. He told her about the Orient Express, its almost decadent luxury that was a startling contrast to today's more spartan rail cars. It had been research, he said, combined with vacation. A kind of reward for finishing his second book and groundwork for the third.

"A third book?" she asked. "What is it called?"

He tried not to stare as she lifted the pansy from her plate and put it into her mouth, her jaw working almost imperceptibly over the soft petals.

That settled the edibility question, he thought. He stared at his own flower and decided to give it a miss anyhow.

"I don't know the title yet," he said. Chapter three wasn't a place to get too attached to a name, even if he'd managed to come up with one. He'd keep a list of possibilities and sift through them when he was done. In the meantime, he told her, it was known as "Untitled, Number Three."

"When will it come out?"

"After I write it, I suppose." Then he surprised himself by telling her about the writer's block that had nearly driven him insane over the past year.

"I thought writer's block was just a way to get out of working," she said, and laughed at his exaggerated grimace.

"It was real enough," he said.

"Was?"

"It's over now."

"I'm glad," she said softly. "I loved *The Seventh Kiss.*"

Hearing her say it gave him a fierce sense of satisfaction, no less potent at that moment than it had been the other night when she'd told him the first time.

"I suppose you'll hit me if I say 'I told you so.'"

"Your instincts are valid," Cassandra said dryly, lowering her lashes as she took a sip of wine. It was vaguely disappointing, his casual acceptance of her praise. One more fan, she supposed. Another affirmation of his talent.

She wanted to be more.

He dropped a kiss on her cheek and murmured "I told you so," into her ear, then retreated to the far side of his seat to avoid retaliation.

She glared at him theatrically, a cover for her rattled senses, and wished he didn't have the power to distract her so easily. It wasn't comforting to know he could reduce her to a mass of quivering nerves with only an innocent kiss on the cheek. She should be more mature by this time in her life, she thought, and able to handle a little kiss. She was thirty-three and widowed. It wasn't as though she was an untried virgin.

It was just that he made her feel like one, all trembly and tingling and nervous, and she wondered if she'd get over that nonsense before he broke her heart.

Cassandra almost choked on her swallow of wine. She hadn't considered her heart before, not in connection with Carlson. She could no longer ignore the truth, though. Her heart was exactly the reason she'd been willing to settle for an affair . . . even though she wanted more.

Her heart. Damn! She sighed and shoved the horrible truth aside. She'd deal with it later, when she was alone.

Or maybe she'd not deal with it at all, because it couldn't possibly be true. Mere attraction didn't involve the heart.

"You certainly don't look like you enjoyed *The Seventh Kiss*," Carlson said. "I think you're making it up."

She shook her head and brought her thoughts back to the Wine Train. His writing, she reminded herself. It was time to make amends for the horrid things she'd said just a few days ago. "I told you. I loved *The Seventh Kiss,* so much so that I even went out and bought *Applause of Angels* today."

"I would have given you a copy if you'd asked."

"That's no way to make a living," she quipped. "How can you expect to get rich if you give away the merchandise?"

He studied her for a long moment, apparently missing the joke entirely. "I suppose that getting rich isn't one of my goals," he finally said.

"Surely rides on the Orient Express don't come cheap?" she asked. She thought he was looking at her a little strangely, but put it down to her imagination.

"That's not rich," he argued. "That's comfortable. I like to be in a position to do what I wish, within reason. And I don't think giving away a couple of books is going to change things by much."

"Then I guess I'll let you give me a copy of your third one, if you're determined to be generous," she said, setting her empty glass on the sill.

"It'll be a while coming. These things take time."

Cassandra knew he was thinking about his writer's block, and she didn't want him to have any doubts. She had none at all when it came to his talent and future. "You will be a successful writer, you know."

Carlson wondered what she'd say if she knew he didn't have to depend on his writing for his living. Thanks to a zealously efficient financial advisor, he'd banked enough over the years to see him through the rest of his life without working another day.

He didn't tell Cassandra that, because as long as she thought he was financially dependent on his writing, she wouldn't get any silly notions that they might, after all, be more compatible than she'd imagined.

"Telling fortunes now?" he asked with a chuckle.

She nodded, a knowing smile on her lips. "There are some things in life that just seem inevitable, and your success is one of them." When he looked at her in patent disbelief, she added, "I suppose you know the story about my namesake, don't you?"

"No."

"The Cassandra prophecy?"

He looked as though he might suddenly recall the ancient myth, but eventually shook his head and shrugged.

In a hushed voice, she related the fable. "The god Apollo loved Cassandra and bestowed the gift of prophecy upon her in exchange for . . . her favors. Cassandra accepted the gift, then spurned Apollo. In his anger, he cursed her."

"What was the curse?"

"Although what she foretold came true, nobody believed her prophecies."

Carlson grinned. "Tell me another one."

"A story?"

"A prophecy."

Cassandra nibbled some cheese to give herself time to think, and almost gave up when she noticed the pansy he'd avoided eating. "I predict you won't die if you eat that pretty little flower," she said brightly.

He laughed. "I guess the prophecy works then, because I don't believe you."

"Well, you should. This one certainly isn't poisonous, although I wouldn't recommend grazing on any pansies you might find in your garden. There are some varieties that might be toxic."

"As in bad for your health?"

"Quite possibly. I don't remember the details." She

grinned, because the image of Carlson foraging for pansies was totally absurd.

"I suppose this means I should be more adventurous," he drawled.

"And here I thought I was the one without a sense of adventure."

Carlson thought about that for a moment. This was a perfect opportunity, he realized, to remind her of how easily she used to blush—something she hadn't done all night. He couldn't resist. "I think I'm already surprised at how . . . adventurous you are," he said with deliberate innuendo. "You've nothing to apologize for."

Her brows knit into an expressive question mark and she asked him what he meant.

Leaning just a fraction closer, he whispered into her ear, "The woman I thought you were wouldn't have let me into her house so late last Friday night, much less allowed me to put my mouth to her breast."

Carlson sat back and watched the flames of self-conscious outrage brighten her cheeks. He felt a comfortable sense of accomplishment that he'd been able to provoke her into a stunned silence. He hadn't lost his touch.

Cassandra fumed for a long moment before she saw the mischief in his eyes . . . and discovered that she'd rather get even than get angry. With less caution than sense, she leaned across the gap between their chairs and put her hand on his thigh. High enough to cause a sudden intake of breath, she noted with satisfaction. But she wasn't done.

Holding his definitely aroused gaze with her own, she murmured, "Don't start what you can't finish. Or won't."

Carlson put his lips to hers before she could add anything, laughter rising in his chest as he tasted her anew and realized what a marvelous time he was having.

Cassandra gave as good as she got.

"Behave, Silk," he said against her mouth, "or I'll have to pull you off the train in St. Helena." He delicately picked up her hand by the wrist and placed it back on her own lap.

She grinned, as much amused by his reaction as she was astonished at her own boldness. Shy? she wondered. Well, maybe tomorrow. "Not before dinner, Carlson. I'm hungry."

He growled deep in his throat and asked her what she thought about *Applause of Angels*. Anything to change the subject.

Cassandra took a moment to slide the pansy into his mouth, deliberately ignoring his exaggerated gagging noises and acting superior when she reminded him of the Cassandra prophecy. But both her fingers burned with the firm touch of his lips, and she knew she was throwing herself into a fire that would burn and scar.

She didn't care.

The book, she reminded herself sternly, and began to share with him her delight in his writing. She admitted she was only halfway through, but she was enjoying it every bit as much as *The Seventh Kiss*. She couldn't help but let her feelings cloud her words as she talked about favorite scenes from both books and why she liked them.

It seemed like forever ago that she'd disparaged his writing without ever having read a single word, a century since she'd fought that battle against letting him see the things he made her feel.

She truly loved his books. And, as she talked, the truth she didn't want to think about began to consume her. She tripped over a couple of words as she faced the realization that something irrevocable was happening to her emotions.

Her heart tripped, too, and she had a hard time keeping her expression innocently unaware. But how could someone be calm about a calamity like *falling in love*!

She'd die before she let him know.

Taking up the threads of her elaborate monologue again, Cassandra wondered if she'd have any better luck hiding her growing love than she'd had hiding the simple attraction she'd felt before.

Six

Dinner was brill.

She told him so over dessert, and he laughed into his coffee.

Cassandra dipped her spoon into his crème caramel, saying she wanted to know if it was as good as the one she made. He told her that was a flimsy excuse for stealing half of his dessert and helped himself to a healthy bite of her chocolate torte.

The entire meal had been like that, full of laughs and smiles as they divulged tales of family and friends, getting to know each other despite a mutual, unspoken resolve to keep a few secrets. It was as though they'd agreed to hold back some essentials, each remembering they were exploring a temporary attraction, nothing permanent.

She wasn't the kind of woman he needed to share his life, Cassandra told herself with recurring persistence.

But as the Wine Train made its way through the moonlit valley and they faced each other across a dazzlingly white linen tablecloth, they probed as far as they dared. And while they paid much less attention than was deserved to the gourmet fare and excellent California wines, Cassandra would have said at any given moment that the evening, to date, was a smashing success.

She enjoyed Carlson's company, and was strangely confident that he enjoyed hers as well. They were good together. Perhaps, she mused, there was a chance for friendship in the end. She didn't know, however, if being his friend might hurt more than never seeing him again.

She didn't want to think about it.

She learned that Carlson had been mostly on his own from his early teens, orphaned by an airplane crash. No relatives stepped forward to take in the child that was becoming a man. A series of foster homes followed, then college because he'd worked hard to earn it, and a commission in the Navy after he received his degree.

He left out a lot of the years following that. Not that he'd been anything more than vague before, she thought with rueful acceptance. He was only going to share so much, not all.

He'd had affairs before, she recognized. He knew the rules. She paid them due attention.

She did ask him how he'd met Mallory. Peggy had told her they'd lived together—nonromantically—for years before Mallory met and married Jake Gallegher, but Cassandra had never heard the story behind it.

"I worked for her father," Carlson said. "I took care of security for his manufacturing operation, and it eventually extended to include his family."

"So how did you end up out here with Mallory?"

"I was ready to start writing. Mallory wanted to get out from under her father's watchful eye."

Cassandra smiled. "I'd imagine that he wouldn't have been too happy with the two of you living together."

"Mallory's father knew me well enough to realize that we were too close to ever let things get complicated that way. Although I have to admit that Jake wasn't as convinced in the beginning." He told her then about Mallory and Jake's romance and his part in helping things along when they got rocky— something about pushing Mallory overboard and making her swim ashore to where Jake was waiting.

Cassandra didn't believe one word of it.

Mallory was as close as he had to family, she realized, and he guarded that bond with a devotion that gave her a glimpse of the love he was capable of. Jake, Mallory's husband, had entered that family circle, and Carlson had welcomed him as a brother.

She envied his pseudosiblings. She'd been raised as an only child, and her parents were more like distant relatives now. They were still in the thick of things on the East Coast, she told Carlson, busy in their frantic social whirl, leaving her to lead her own life in the San Francisco Bay Area without much, if any, interference.

"They tried to get me to come home after Michael died," she said. "But I didn't want to leave California. Mother made a fuss for a couple of months, telling me how much she needed me, what with the Hunt Ball coming up and the Christmas festivities just around the corner."

"Your mother entertains a lot?"

"Mm. Seems like she's always had one thing or another in the works. I can't remember a time when I didn't know how to set the table for a formal dinner or which wine to serve with fish." She smiled because the memories were good ones: She'd loved learning the ins and outs of entertaining.

"I guess that's where you learned which fork to use," Carlson said dryly.

She laughed. "But naturally. And that was the easy

part." She went on, explaining how her mother had spent the better part of her days coping with the demands of her father's career—a cocktail party for the new vice president, coffee with the Junior League, charity balls for a multitude of causes, for just a few examples.

"She planned each detail and then took me through every inch of it from the time my attention span exceeded five minutes. Mother taught me everything from arranging flowers to where to seat the ex-wife of the new governor, both of whom might be there with their current spouses."

"Where *do* you seat her?"

"Why, I suppose it depends upon a number of things, but I personally prefer to seat them together so they can show everyone how well they've adjusted to the divorce."

"What if they start to tear strips off each other in the middle of the main course?"

"If there had been any danger of that happening, I wouldn't have had them at the same party in the first place," she said, a note of surprise in her voice at his ignorant query.

Carlson accepted the implied reprimand with a grin and reached for the silver coffeepot. "So I guess there's more to giving a party than sending out invitations and cooking the food."

"A bit," she said mildly, but didn't expand on it. It wasn't as though it was a real job she could brag about, and she wished she hadn't said as much as she already had.

"What do you think I should do with myself instead?" she asked to change the subject. "Program computers? Drive a truck? Write a column for the local newspaper?"

"I imagine you might not be qualified for any of those."

"I've wanted to try something else, pursue a real career," she said, and lowered her gaze when she saw the flash of disbelief in his eyes. "But I can't seem to settle on anything that doesn't take a lot of training. And whenever I get ambitious about it, someone calls and asks me to do a party or dinner or whatever, and then I don't have time to worry about my alternatives."

"You could always say no," he suggested.

"I know." She looked up so that she could watch him as she gave him the complete truth. "The trouble is, I don't *want* to. I really like organizing parties for people."

"You want to be a hostess for the rest of your life?"

"Yes, I rather think so." She saw the censure in his expression and it reaffirmed what she already knew. Carlson had no respect for a woman who couldn't get out in the world and be truly independent. Stirring her coffee even though there was nothing to stir because she took it black, she held his gaze and added, "Either privately, if I marry again, or as I do now. Organizing parties is what I do best."

"You don't think you'd continue working if you remarried?"

"There wouldn't be any need," she said simply. "If it's anything like my marriage to Michael, I'd be too busy handling my own entertaining to do any for other people."

And that, she decided, took care of that subject. Too bad she couldn't lie and make up better answers. That wouldn't solve anything, though. She couldn't change who she really was.

"How long before the money runs out?" he asked bluntly.

She grinned, and that clearly took him aback.

"According to Dennis, my trusty accountant, the money Michael left me is intact and will probably remain that way as long as I continue at this level of business."

"You're self-supporting?"

"I guess that's one way of putting it. Dennis said that I've already replaced the capital I used right after Michael died, and that I can sit back and watch it multiply as long as business continues as it has this past year." She crossed her fingers under the table. There was no guarantee her streak of good luck would last forever, and it scared her witless to imagine a life without something to do. Entertaining was all she knew.

Carlson appeared stunned. "You're not taking anything out of whatever money your husband left?"

"Not in the last year, anyway," she said, proud that she could brag a little about this. It wasn't as though she was a *real* businesswoman or anything. But she felt a certain pride in knowing she was making a living at what she'd been raised to do as a matter of course. "Dennis says I can even buy my own shoes now."

She kicked her foot into the aisle, wiggling it until he leaned over to look. Grinning at his puzzled expression, she couldn't resist boasting. "I bought these with my own money. And the dress. *After* I paid the mortgage and utilities and everything else."

It dawned on Carlson that he'd been wrong about more than one thing when it came to the petite blonde in the knockout dress across the table.

Cassandra wasn't shy. She just thought she was. And even though he'd told her differently, she hadn't believed him.

Cassandra wasn't clingy. He'd just seen the physical image of his ex-wife and imagined that was the case.

Cassandra wasn't dependent on anyone, least of all a husband. She was self-supporting and doing something she enjoyed. Even if he felt hosting parties for friends was a rather flimsy excuse for making a living, it worked.

No, she wasn't dependent at all . . . and the only person that didn't know it was Cassandra.

As the train pulled into the Napa station, Carlson was wondering how best to reveal to her the little secrets that she kept from herself.

Cassandra's laughter filled the car as the limousine turned south on Highway 29. "I *told* you we shouldn't get that picture taken, but no, you just had to insist!"

"You wouldn't be laughing if it was you standing there with your eyes closed and mouth half-open," Carlson grumbled, and snatched the photo from her fingers. He looked like a certified idiot, but he tried to look at the positive side of it. At least he had a picture of Cassandra. A good one, too, even if she had been a reluctant model.

He couldn't wait to cut his half of the photo to shreds. She was still laughing as he tucked the semi-offensive image into his breast pocket.

Her laughter continued when he offered her a cognac, which she refused. Flicking off the interior lights after pouring a small measure for himself, he tasted the cognac, then set the glass aside as Cassandra tried to control her giggles. She still didn't stop when he threatened to put a muzzle on her, so he went ahead and did it.

Carlson stilled her laughs with his mouth, taking advantage of her parted lips to thrust his tongue inside her mouth where it was warm and wet. He stroked and demanded, tasting her fire as she quivered under the assault of his lips. She moaned, a soft cry that he took into his own mouth as he gentled his kiss.

She didn't want gentle.

Cassandra advanced when he retreated, her fingers grasping the lapels of his jacket as she lifted herself closer to his mouth. She felt more than heard his harsh groan of surprise, and knew that she had won when he returned with a thrusting rhythm that sent her reeling with delight.

His mouth left hers to nudge back the long silky curls, revealing her ear. Then he ignored it in favor of the satiny skin just below it. He kissed and nibbled and laughed because it was his turn now, and it gave him so much pleasure to feel her squirm with frustration against him.

She slipped her arms under his jacket and tried to pull him close, then nipped his chin when he resisted. Carlson chuckled and returned his lips to hers before she could do any real damage. He brushed her mouth with his mustache, and she moaned and told him she loved it, the feel of the soft bristles on her lips.

Then he murmured erotic suggestions about other areas that might be susceptible to his mustache. A cry of anticipation escaped her lips as she gave her imagination free rein. Her fingers dug into the firm muscles of his back, and struggled to free her legs so that she could wrap them around his hips.

Carlson denied her struggles because he understood exactly what she was seeking to do. He would have no control, if she did that. Backseat or not, he wouldn't have the strength to resist.

He took a deep breath and tried for gentle again, and he was persistent this time. It was the only chance of holding back the tide of their passion. The fierce demand of her hungry kisses nearly swayed him, but Carlson had made up his mind.

"I'm not going to take you in the backseat of a

limo," he murmured in between swiping licks of his tongue across her lips.

"No?"

"Uh-uh."

"Never?" she asked, fighting his efforts to pull her arms from around his waist. She compromised, dragging her nails across his back as he tugged at her hands, then taking the opportunity to push her fingers into his hair.

He chuckled, then covered her mouth with a satisfying wet kiss before pulling her hands away. Abruptly he threw himself into the opposite corner. Never had he wanted a woman more.

And never had he wanted it to be so perfect. For that reason alone, he was willing to wait. The backseat of a limousine might be an exciting rendezvous for lovers, but with Cassandra, he wanted to take his time.

He wanted her naked and writhing beneath him.

He wanted lights so that he could watch her face as he touched her where she was swollen and wet and waiting for him to make them one.

He wanted to give her romance, not merely lust.

Cassandra gazed across the dark expanse of seat and wished she could see his face. She needed to know if he was as uncomfortable as she.

She wanted him more than ever.

She loved him, and because saying so was out of the question, she wanted to show him in a way he wouldn't fathom.

She wanted to show her love with her body so that in the reality of loving him, she could find some sort of peace after he was gone. There would be comfort in the memories of what they'd shared.

Making love with Carlson would mean different things to each of them, she knew without a single doubt. But it was something she needed to do.

Passion awaits you...
Step into the magical world of
Loveswept

A Magical World of Enchantment Awaits You When You're Loveswept!

Your heart will be swept away with Loveswept Romances when you meet exciting heroes you'll fall in love with...beautiful heroines you'll identify with. Share the laughter, tears and the passion of unforgettable couples as love works its magic spell. These romances will lift you into the exciting world of love, charm and enchantment!

You'll enjoy award-winning authors such as Iris Johansen, Sandra Brown, Kay Hooper and others who top the best-seller lists. Each offers a kaleidoscope of adventure and passion that will enthrall, excite and exhilarate you with the magic of being Loveswept!

- ♥ *We'd like to send you 6 new novels to enjoy—risk free!*
- ♥ *There's no obligation to buy.*
- ♥ *6 exciting romances—plus your free gift—brought right to your door!*
- ♥ *Convenient money-saving, time-saving home delivery!*

Join the Loveswept at-home reader service and we'll send you 6 new romances about once a month— before they appear in the bookstore! You always get 15 days to preview them before you decide. Keep only those you want. Each book is yours for only $2.25*. That's a total savings of $3.00 off the retail price for each 6 book shipment.

*plus shipping & handling and sales tax in NY and Canada

Enjoy 6 Romances–Risk Free! Plus...
An Exclusive Romance Novel Free!

Detach and mail card today!

Loveswept

AFFIX RISK FREE BOOK STAMP HERE.

Yes! Please send my 6 Loveswept novels RISK FREE along with the exclusive romance novel "Larger Than Life" as my <u>free gift</u> to keep.

RA 412 28

NAME

ADDRESS   APT.

CITY

STATE   ZIP

MY "NO RISK"
Guarantee

I understand when I accept your offer for Loveswept Romances I'll receive the 6 newest Loveswept novels right at home about once a month (before they're in bookstores!). I'll have 15 days to look them over. If I don't like the books, I'll simply return them and owe nothing. You even pay the return postage. Otherwise, I'll pay just $2.25 per book (plus shipping & handling & sales tax in NY and Canada). I *save* $3.00 off the retail price of the 6 books! I understand there's no obligation to buy and I can cancel anytime. No matter what, the gift is mine to keep–*free!*

SEND NO MONEY NOW. Prices subject to change. Orders subject to approval

ENJOY...

♥ 6 Romance Novels–Risk Free! ♥ Exclusive Novel Free!
♥ Money Saving Home Delivery!

FREE BOOK OFFER
RUSH!

BUSINESS REPLY MAIL

FIRST CLASS MAIL   PERMIT NO. 2456   HICKSVILLE, NY

POSTAGE WILL BE PAID BY ADDRESSEE

Loveswept

BANTAM BOOKS
P.O. BOX 985
HICKSVILLE, NY 11802-9827

NO POSTAGE
NECESSARY
IF MAILED
IN THE
UNITED STATES

"Always an excuse," she said lightly, finding the courage to act the part he required of her—sophisticated and emotionally apart. "If it's not one thing, then it's another."

"Don't pout, Silk," he said, and reached across to take her hand in his. "It's only another thirty minutes or so."

Thirty minutes to worry about it, she thought, sighing silently. Her house or his? Would he expect her just to strip down and jump into bed, or would he prefer to help? What if she didn't please him? What if she was too nervous?

What if he changed his mind?

She fidgeted and wished she knew more about what she was getting into. An affair was so different from marriage, she realized. The demands had to be different, and the expectations as well.

"Silk?"

"Yes?"

"There's nothing to be nervous about. You don't even have to make up your mind until we get there."

"How did you know?"

"That you're nervous?"

"Yes."

"Besides your cold hand and the way you keep shivering, you mean?"

She giggled, then sighed in relief as he tugged at her hand until she was sitting close. He put his arm around her shoulders, and she snuggled into the warmth of his reassurance. Threading her fingers through his, she took pleasure in their joined hands resting on his hard thigh.

"Carlson?"

"Mm?"

"My house is closer."

He reached for the cognac he'd poured earlier and

tossed it down his throat. Control was easier said than done.

Carlson dismissed the driver at Cassandra's and told Cassandra he'd take a taxi home.

"You're already planning on leaving?" she asked as she dug her keys out of her purse and handed them to him.

"In five minutes or at five in the morning," he said without any indication of which he preferred. "However it turns out." He pushed the key into the lock, then moved aside to allow her to precede him. She stepped inside the house, her hands twisting the strap of her purse, and stopped in the center of the cold hall, wondering what the hell she was supposed to do now.

"Cassandra?" His nearness startled her, his voice a low murmur just behind her. She would have turned, but he put his hands on her shoulders, a light touch that persuaded her not to move. His fingers dragged the heavy length of her hair off her shoulders, and the cool air brought goose bumps to her skin.

"Cassandra!" he said again, impatiently this time.

"Yes?" Her voice quavered in the silent house, and she wished she were better at this. Cool and confident, like Carlson.

Practiced, so she wouldn't make a fool of herself.

"What are you wearing under that dress?"

She gasped, then cried her pleasure aloud as his mouth grazed the sensitive nerves at her nape. She almost collapsed into his embrace as his arms came around her from behind, and his hands began their own exploration in lieu of her response. Their bodies came together, front to back. Feeling his hard arousal against her, she rejoiced in the knowledge that he wanted her as completely as a man could want a woman.

He wanted her now.

"Lace," he said with a grunt of approval, feeling the edge of her bra beneath the thin silk of her dress. His tongue darted a wet path along her hairline to the rim of her ear as he cupped her breasts, massaging them with firm, circling motions.

Cassandra's breathing was shallow and fast, and her fingers grabbed at his forearms for support. She couldn't rely on her legs to stay beneath her. They were growing less supportive by the moment, with his every kiss and touch. She murmured her objections when he gently removed her hands, saying something about the freedom to explore and how he couldn't do it very well if she was hanging onto him.

"But I can hardly stand up," she said in gasps when his hands returned to fondle her breasts. "My legs are like rubber."

"You want to try the floor?" he teased, nipping her earlobe.

"It's marble—"

Choking off an expletive that would have shocked the very proper woman in his arms, Carlson pulled her hands down and back a little, shoving them into his jacket pockets, out of the way. Then he braced her body against his and told her to lean back, to let him take her weight. She complied without hesitation, and his fingers returned to the beaded nipples. He discovered he liked this new position, Cassandra's small but perfect breasts thrusting out into his hands. Her growing passion was evident in the frequent gasps and moans that spilled from her lips.

Carlson wanted her to scream her pleasure.

His hands smoothed down her dress, pushing her coat aside and delving inside to trace the line of her waist. He almost lost himself in the heat of her skin through the silk, then bent forward, his hands seeking. It would have been easier if he turned her around, so that he could find the hem of her skirt and pull it to her hips, out of the way.

He didn't, though. It was more exciting this way, with Cassandra melting into his chest, her body open to his whim.

She gave a little scream when he laid his palm firmly on her quivering belly, and he smiled as he soothed her with words of promise and patience, then let his fingers explore lower. "Panties, garters, and stockings," he whispered with delight. "What color, Cassandra?"

She couldn't possibly answer him, not when his hands were pulling at her thighs so that she would part them . . . especially not when his fingers caressed her through her dress until she knew that he could feel her wet response.

She couldn't possibly answer him, and he growled his approval at her aroused silence. "I suppose I'll know soon enough," he murmured. His hand cupped her jaw and tugged her head back against his shoulder, then he pushed his tongue into her mouth and devoured her, his hunger all-pervasive, his control forgotten and not missed.

"You kiss like a wanton," he said between nips at her lips. Then he nearly came apart when she sucked his tongue into her mouth and stroked it with her teeth.

"You make me forget that I'm a shy person," she said breathlessly a few moments later, and he swept his hand from breast to thigh in praise of who she was, telling her silently how much he enjoyed touching her.

She said she wanted to touch him too.

"Bed, I think," he muttered.

She protested because she didn't want to wait to climb the stairs.

He reminded her about the marble floor and swept her into his arms.

Beneath the sky blue canopy of her four-poster bed, Carlson led Cassandra with delicacy and laughter through the intimate intricacies of making love with a man for the first time. He taught her what he liked, and learned what pleased her the most.

Everything, she told him, and laughed when he wiggled his mustache and told her he'd take that as a personal dare.

She didn't have to worry about who took off whose clothes and in what order. It happened without thinking, a piece at a time, and it didn't matter to whom each piece belonged. Carlson dragged out the process, finding delight in the secrets of her lingerie.

"I didn't imagine you'd wear black," he murmured huskily as he tried for the second time to catch his breath.

"You like it?"

"Mm." And he showed her that he wasn't kidding.

They finally lay naked atop the sheets, and when she shivered it wasn't from the cold. Carlson wrapped her in his embrace, discovering that petite didn't mean fragile. Cassandra was strong in her response to his every caress, fighting to give when he would rather she only take.

She demanded he bend to her will, and he pleasurably suffered the caress of her mouth as she practiced a few erotic tricks. He knew he'd never again look at her lips without remembering.

Carlson displaced her from her position of dominance before she pushed him beyond a point of no return, hushing her complaints with promises of getting even. He proceeded to do so, and took his own enjoyment in her taste . . . and in the titillating picture of Cassandra straining toward and against the strokes of his hands and mouth. Her fingers dug into the mattress beneath her, her head tossed against the mound of pillows, and her body arched beneath his every caress.

She was enthusiastic about his imaginative use of his mustache and giggled for a long time before he showed her just how creative he could get. Then she screamed her pleasure.

He showed her the stars in the heavens and cuddled her gently when she fell from orbit . . . then he launched her again over her protests that she couldn't breathe in outer space.

He held himself from her for as long as was humanly possible, making it better, he told her.

She told him she wanted to be conscious when he took his own pleasure, if he didn't mind.

He didn't mind at all.

He wanted her never to forget how good they were together, because he knew the memory of making love with Cassandra would stay with him forever.

Seven

It was closer to seven than five when he left her the next morning.

Carlson pushed one arm into his jacket and picked up the telephone with the other hand, completing the awkward process of dressing and summoning a taxi at the same time because he was in a hurry. Twenty minutes, the voice on the phone told him.

"Why so early?" Cassandra mumbled from the bed where she lay pretty much hidden among a chaotic jumble of pillows.

"Work," he said with humor in his voice. "And I seem to remember your saying you had a brunch or something today."

"Ugh." Even though she knew Sonia would be walking in the door at eight or earlier, Cassandra wasn't in the mood to think about it.

She didn't want the night to be over. But then, she *never* wanted the night to be over. She loved to sleep.

Carlson found his shoes by the door and looked around for his socks, spotting them in a pile with Cassandra's garter belt and stockings.

Flashbacks of the night before almost stole his

resolve to leave. But he had to. They wouldn't have the house to themselves much longer.

"Wake up, Cass," he ordered as sternly as he could. One of them had to be strong, and he'd realized a few minutes earlier that it was going to have to be him. If getting the day started had been left to Cassandra, he wouldn't already be up and dressed.

He'd be lying with her under the covers, testing her will to sleep and cuddle against his need to be deep inside her again.

"Sure," Cassandra said, and snuggled deeper.

Carlson took his shoes and socks over to a chair by the window and pulled them on, his gaze searching for her shape under the sheets and blankets and pillows. He recognized a lump that might have been her charming little tush and was instantly aroused by visions of his hands cupping her to him. The hot words of their passion flooded over him as he remembered her frenzied response, and he felt himself harden in renewed desire.

He wanted her now, before she was quite awake. She would be toasty warm within her burrow, his hands like ice against her skin.

The contrast sparked his imagination.

Unfortunately, reason asserted itself when his glance caught the time on her bedside clock. "Get up, Cassandra! Now!"

Up. What a miserable word, Cassandra thought. She squelched her inclination to ignore him, knowing he wouldn't go away until she made an effort. Tossing back the covers, she hugged a soft down pillow to her chest for warmth and rose up on her knees, half out of bed and half not. She wasn't a morning person, and getting up was normally accomplished in stages. Making it as far as her knees on the first try was close to a record. Most mornings, she usually only managed to throw back the covers before the coolness of the room sent her scurrying under them again.

This wasn't most mornings, she admitted with gradual recall, and her eyes focused blearily on the man who had given her the most exciting night of her life. She felt her body quicken as she remembered detail after detail of the preceding hours. If she hadn't been so sleepy, she might have tried to coerce him back into bed.

Making love with Carlson had been terrifyingly exquisite . . . terrifying because she knew she'd never experience such dramatic heights with another man.

Carlson carefully folded his tie and tucked it into his jacket pocket before allowing himself to look at her again. His breath wedged in his throat as he absorbed her unconsciously erotic pose, and he knew he'd been foolish to look at her at all.

Hair all atangle, eyes half-open, and her face slightly puffy from sleep, Cassandra was more tempting without even trying than any other woman would be in full seduction mode.

He didn't want to leave.

Staring across the room at the fully dressed man who looked disgustingly wide awake, Cassandra stifled an impulse to throw something.

"Are you a morning person?" she asked suspiciously, pushing back the hair that spilled over her eyes.

He looked away. "Sometimes." The taxi would arrive in ten minutes or so, and he couldn't afford to surrender to the urge to throw off his clothes and tackle her. Instead he studied the room that was inoffensively feminine in the half-light of the early morning. An oriental carpet in soft pastel colors stretched from wall to wall, atop which stood the enormous canopied bed, a couple of bedside tables, two flower-patterned chairs, and a dressing table. The bathroom adjoined through one door, and he'd found a comfortably sized dressing room through the other when he'd been looking for the bathroom.

He liked the way she'd kept from cluttering the bedroom with extra furniture, and envied the large rooms she had to work with. His houseboat was elegant and functional, but it didn't have the luxury of space that Cassandra's Victorian residence afforded.

"I like your home," he said as he picked up her panties from the rug and laid them on the chair where he'd earlier draped her dress. "I envy your elbow room."

"I've heard your houseboat isn't exactly a hovel." She yawned, wondering if she should at least get up and offer him coffee. No, she decided. He looked ready to leave, and coffee would only slow his exit.

Maybe when she woke up, that would bother her. At the moment, though, she was reluctantly concentrating on trying to wake up. Her natural unwillingness to face the morning was compounded by a shortage of sleep that was almost criminal. Carlson's fault, she judged without malice. She yawned again, blinking back tears that had filled eyes that she knew were red and puffy. Lordy, but she hated getting up!

Her alarm sounded and she automatically hit the snooze button, calculating how long it would take her to shower and dress. Sonia was due in less than an hour, and there was a brunch at eleven. Everything she hadn't taken care of yesterday would have to be done before then.

She figured she could sneak another ten minutes' sleep.

"Cassandra?"

"Hm?" She looked up to find Carlson standing

beside the bed, just a foot or so away. She smiled, a sleepy recognition of his presence, and rubbed her eyes.

"You're going back to sleep the moment I walk out the door, aren't you?" he asked as he reached toward her, his knuckles a rough caress across her cheeks.

"Um-hm." She leaned into the caress and closed her eyes. Having Carlson around to wake up to put a whole new light on the morning, she thought with her eyes firmly shut against the encroaching day.

"Silk?"

"Hm?"

"Do you wonder why you aren't feeling just a tad awkward about things?"

"What things?" she murmured, stretching her neck to encourage his touch.

"Things like waking up with a man in your bedroom. For someone who, by her own admission, hasn't slept with a man in five years, you're remarkably nonchalant about it."

"If I was awake, I'd probably agree with you," she said, and giggled when he tweaked her ear. She could have told him that it hadn't occurred to her to worry about it one way or the other. Waking up to Carlson was the most natural thing in the world.

"Your cast of minions is going to arrive before you even get your eyes open," he warned. "And my taxi is going to be here any second now."

"So go downstairs and wait for it," she mumbled, feeling much like a cat as she enjoyed his light caress on her face and neck. She was just considering curling back up under the covers when his hand stroked across her shoulders and down her back.

Petting of another sort, she thought with a murmur of approval, arching her back as his fingers played their way up her spine. Oh, but that felt good, his fingers slightly calloused and so unbelievably gentle on her skin. She moaned her budding arousal when he put his lips on her shoulder, and didn't argue at all when he tugged the pillow from her arms. She raised her hands to his shoulders and raked her nails down his back, remembering he liked that.

Carlson threw the pillow aside and gave himself just a moment to review the delicious shape of her breasts, the curling tuft of golden blond hair down below. He hadn't meant to start anything, but she'd been so placid under his touch, almost purring her contentment as he'd stroked her face.

It seemed unfair that she could be so peacefully content when he was hard and burning for her.

She was such a temptress, kneeling before him on the bed, her head thrown back as he nibbled his way across her shoulder and down to the curve of her breast. He wanted her, badly, and knew there wasn't time.

Teasing her like this wasn't fair, he conceded, but fair wasn't always how things worked out. He'd be aroused and cursing most of the morning, and he wanted her to share a little of his frustration. He'd make it up to her that night. All night, if he could only keep her awake.

He gave himself a minute. Then he'd leave. Taking a deep breath and hoping the taxi would honk when it arrived, he covered one already hardening nipple with his mouth. He felt her shudder with pleasure, and bit down gently on the velvet tip.

She cried out softly, just as she had time and time again throughout the night. He laughed against her skin, so very pleased with this incredibly sensual woman he'd discovered beneath the serene and re-served Cassandra. His mouth moved to her other breast as his fingers parted the folds of her woman-hood, and he discovered that she was as ready for him as she could be. He stroked her, circled and pushed inside, and she pulled his mouth hard against her breast in her pleasure.

His hand flew to his belt and had almost slipped the buckle when a loud beep from outside stilled his intentions. He let fly a few appropriate adjectives that had nothing to do with the taxi and everything to do with his shortsightedness. He should have known he couldn't touch Cassandra that way without wanting her again.

"Sorry, Silk," he murmured, hushing her protests with his lips. His fingers gave her wet heat a final stroke before he backed away from the bed. "Tonight?"

A blurred vision of Carlson swam into sight as Cassandra tried to focus. "Tonight?" she repeated, knowing that was an impossible amount of time to wait.

She needed him now.

"Tonight," he confirmed. "I'll call you later." He dragged a corner of the sheet up to cover her, saying he couldn't walk away with her kneeling there naked, her body all flushed and ready for whatever he wanted. "Perhaps we could take in a play," he proposed after clearing his throat.

"Or we could just stay here." Cassandra made the suggestion without a thought about how it might sound, but she was too aroused and frustrated to care.

He laughed. "Whatever gave you the idea you're shy, Silk?"

"You've said that before."

"I know." Pausing at her bedroom door, he added, "Think about it. Maybe it's not the only thing you're not that you think you are."

"Excuse me?"

" 'Bye, love." He grinned and left her bedroom.

"Your syntax is appalling, Carlson," she shouted

after his receding footsteps. "How can I think about it if I can't even follow whatever it was you said?" She heard the front door slam and realized that was as good an answer as she was going to get.

Flopping back on the bed, she briefly considered the feasibility of shutting her eyes for a quick forty winks, but the snooze alarm clicked into gear and whined for her attention.

Cassandra smashed the button with her fist and grumbled all the way to the shower. Ten minutes later, as she stood in front of the mirror blow-drying her hair, she decided that if Carlson was going to be so blasted wide awake and cheerful in the mornings, he could at least bring her a cup of coffee.

She'd tell him that tonight, she decided, and began to hum off-key as she thought about the night past . . . and the night to come.

It took Carlson an hour to add the previous night's erotic adventure to his computer file of sensual episodes. He even included the last scene that morning, its frustrating lack of completion still vivid in his thoughts.

Unlike the first couple of scenes, which he'd intended to put in his book, this writing was explicit and factual, picture-perfect recall of the events of the night. He described what happened without any attempt at camouflage. He even used her name—Cassandra—as well as Silk and a variety of other lover's expressions.

Satisfied with his work, Carlson scrolled back to the beginning of the file—the part he'd created that first night he'd kissed her—and began to fiddle with it, getting rid of fiction and replacing it with fact.

The end product was a tantalizing narration of his affair, to date, with Cassandra Lockland.

After saving the file, he removed it from the electronically arranged folder labeled Book Three, Untitled. It was easy to manipulate these pages to a new folder with a new name, The Cassandra File. He copied the new file onto a diskette, and smiled as he popped it out of the computer and wrote The Cassandra File across the top. Whistling, he opened a desk drawer and filed the diskette among an assortment of others holding miscellaneous story ideas, letters, and records.

For his eyes only.

What happened between himself and Cassandra was no longer something he was willing to share. He realized that he was probably overreacting, that Cassandra wouldn't have recognized the much-doctored replay of their sensual encounters had he put them in the new book. But he would have known.

Heaving a sigh of relief at having separated the reality of his life from the fiction of his writing, Carlson tapped a couple of keys and returned to Book Three, Untitled.

His fingers flew over the keyboard but couldn't quite keep up with the creative inventions of his mind, and the corner of his mouth curved in a satisfied smile.

They went to a play that night after all, a production of *Cat on a Hot Tin Roof* by a local repertory company. Afterwards, they returned to her home, where Carlson proceeded to convince Cassandra that she wasn't shy, not even a little bit. •

"Perhaps I'm just not shy around you," she suggested with a daring grin, tugging his hand away from the knot of his tie because she wanted to undo it herself.

He didn't have anything to say to that, not wanting

to think about Cassandra and other men, and whether or not she would be as wildly exciting a wanton in their arms as she was in his.

"A shy woman wouldn't impulsively do a striptease—to classical music, no less—just because her lover had mentioned that he might enjoy watching her undress." He rested his hands on the already heated skin of her waist. She was utterly naked beneath the bright lights of the kitchen, standing on tiptoe with complete disregard for modesty as she struggled with the knot.

She laughed deep in her throat and told him that only the music had been an impulse.

Cassandra had programmed her emotions for fun that night, and all the nights that followed. She wanted to enjoy Carlson in every way, and if that meant dispensing with her inhibitions for the time being, then she was determined to do it. And because the role of the uninhibited woman was so incredibly easy to perform for him, she finally admitted that the word "shy" no longer applied to her.

He rewarded her with a sexy nightgown he'd purchased in a local boutique. It was a delicate, lacy concoction that was the exact color of her skin. When he asked her to put it on she actually blushed, a reminder of times gone by, before dashing into her dressing room. Then she vamped her way across the bedroom to the chair where he waited, all shyness forgotten as she languidly posed and pirouetted, until he captured her wrist and pulled her onto his lap.

When she saw the flames of desire in his eyes, she vowed she'd never forget the pleasure of knowing that he had once wanted her as much as she wanted him.

In the two weeks since the magical journey to Napa Valley, they were apart only to accede to the demands of their work. Carlson told her that his writing was coming along fast and furious, and that he had a hunch it was the best work he'd ever done. Cassandra's heart swelled with pride as she shared in his excitement, and she prayed fervently that she'd still be with him when the book was done.

He gave her no clues, though, as to how long he expected their affair to last.

Her own schedule was frantic, but she squeezed in time for Carlson whenever possible, even going so far as to forfeit an occasional hour or more of her early morning sleep in favor of spending the time with him.

It was a sacrifice he fully understood, Carlson said after his first experience of trying to roust her out of bed just ten minutes before absolutely necessary. It had taken all of the ten minutes to convince her to come out from under the covers, then the alarm had gone off. She'd hit the snooze button and dived back under. Carlson had given up easily, burrowing under the covers to find her and finally, after much convincing, awaking her to a robust round of lovemaking that had made them both late for the day.

Getting her up an hour before the alarm sounded took determination and a lot of planning—and Cassandra discovered certain devious traits in Carlson that she'd never before suspected.

One night when she was fast asleep, he set the clock ahead one hour. She'd raced out of bed and was in the shower before he revealed the truth.

Needless to say, Cassandra took steps to make sure that trick only worked once.

Another morning, he stripped the covers from the bed and threw them out the bedroom door, leaving her to shiver atop the mattress. That succeeded in waking her up, although he later confessed that her mood wasn't the most pleasant he'd experienced.

She'd hit him on her way to the bathroom, then stood under the shower until the hot water turned to tepid. Naturally, she'd showered first, leaving Carlson a quick rinse or a bad case of the shivers. His choice, she offered when he shouted his outrage under the stinging spray.

They went out for breakfast a lot because it was something he loved doing, although he admitted to becoming quite fond of breakfast in bed, cuisine à la Cassandra.

Even with all the nights they managed to spend together, there were several that they couldn't—Cassandra's parties being the cause of this enforced separation. She thought Carlson was being surprisingly forbearing about the occasional late nights that she had to work . . . until the night she called him just after midnight to explain that she would rather he didn't come over afterwards as planned. The party wasn't over yet, she told him, and then there was still all the cleanup and really, she'd be less anxious about it if she knew she wasn't keeping him awake.

Carlson's facade of indulgent patience cracked, and Cassandra learned just how little tolerance he had for her parties.

In a word, none.

He curtly told her that he'd be there in an hour and if she didn't want her guests to see him, then she should call an end to the night's festivities before he arrived. It took all her skill to encourage the last guests to leave, and that was just moments before Carlson strode boldly up the walk. In front of her staff, he kissed her with unself-conscious hunger, then mounted the stairs to wait for her in her bedroom.

After that evening, Cassandra made it a point to wind up her entertaining activities well in advance of the early morning hours.

On one of her nights off, Carlson took her to the showing of a new artist at Mallory's gallery. They wandered hand in hand through the crowded rooms and discovered that neither of them had any appreciation at all for the surrealist paintings on the walls. Mallory told them they obviously had no taste because she'd already sold six and they'd been open less than an hour.

Then she eyed their joined hands with appropriate speculation and asked for a report. Carlson hugged her in farewell after telling her to mind her own business, a less than subtle hint that did nothing to stop Mallory from calling Cassandra bright and early the next morning.

Cassandra told her the same thing as Carlson, though more tactfully. When she hung up the telephone, she informed the man nibbling on her toes that she was getting hungry herself, and what were they having for breakfast?

He grinned wickedly and bit a slow, wet path up her legs until she forgot the question.

They made love frequently, always passionately, and never in haste.

When they were apart, Cassandra found herself alternately exhilarated and depressed.

She loved being with Carlson, and hated the thought that it must eventually come to an end.

Not really an end, she corrected herself. More like a shift in emphasis. Carlson would eventually stop calling. They would agree that it was over, thanks for the good times, good-bye. He'd go back to the familiar rhythms of his life, releasing Cassandra to return to hers. Except that her life would never be the same.

It would be empty, and yet filled with images of a love she couldn't have, scenes from an affair that had captured her heart.

• • •

Cassandra stared at her surroundings and wondered how Carlson could have said the houseboat lacked elbow room. The living room where she stood accommodated two small groupings of sofas and easy chairs, one set facing the fireplace, the other fronting a bay window. Eye-pleasing ice blue and mint green fabrics lent an agreeably misty feel to the room, with bright splashes of color adding a comfortable warmth.

"You gave me the impression you were a little cramped here," she said dryly, accepting the glass of soda water Carlson handed her.

He shrugged, then took her free hand and led her over to the large bay window. Pulling her down onto the sofa beside him, he threw his arm around her shoulders. It felt right, having her close. "This room is okay," he said. "But the bedrooms are on the small side. And my office would fit into your closet."

She laughed and told him her dressing room/closet was a necessity she'd created out of frustration. "I used to use most of the closets in the house for my clothes. It was a pain having to run to one room for a blouse and another for a skirt. A while after Michael died, I had the small guest room next to the master suite converted into what is now my dressing room and closet."

"You have a lot of clothes," he said with mild amusement, then added that it was all right with him. He liked everything she wore, not the least of which was the pale blue cashmere sweater and slacks she had on that night.

She looked fabulous, as usual, and he'd told her that when he picked her up. Still, he wished she'd left her hair down instead of twisting it into a neat chignon. He'd have to do something about that, he decided, and looked forward to taking out the pins, one by one, letting the silk flow through his fingers as he freed it.

"I have a lot of clothes," she agreed, obviously missing the speculative gleam in his eyes. "But it's mostly because I can't throw anything away. These, for example"—she plucked at the slacks—"I've had for eight years. I remember buying them on a trip to New York. With this sweater."

"Good thing you don't gain weight," he murmured, his gaze wandering over the soft curve of her breasts beneath the clinging knit. He approved.

"Don't be silly," she said. "I've got a whole rack of things to accommodate the post-holiday expansion."

"Post-holiday expansion?"

She nodded. "The extra eight pounds that arrive with the Christmas turkey and stick around until that little twirp of a groundhog decides it's spring," she said with resignation in her voice. "And they're the same pounds every year. I recognize them."

Carlson nuzzled her ear and said he was looking forward to making their acquaintance, then added a couple of lewd suggestions about possible means of exercising them away as he began to explore the ivory buttons that held her sweater together.

Cassandra's heart soared. Christmas was months away. She pretended she hadn't heard, though, and swatted his roving hands. "Don't forget we've got company in the kitchen." She nodded toward the two large oriental panels that concealed the dining area. The kitchen where Vincent was preparing their feast was just beyond the elegant mahogany table she'd seen earlier.

"I'm beginning to think inviting him over to cook wasn't my brightest idea," Carlson muttered.

"Invite? It was my understanding that there was a bit of arm-twisting going on." Cassandra finished her soda water and leaned forward to put the glass on the low table in front of the sofa. "Care to tell me what you've got on him that made him so pliable?"

Carlson chuckled, then told her how he'd threatened to expose Vincent's behind the scenes machinations which had resulted in Mallory—his boss's wife—being invited to participate in a local charity tennis tournament. She hadn't been able to refuse, since it was for charity.

"What's the catch?" Cassandra asked.

"She doesn't play tennis." Carlson laughed aloud, then explained between chuckles, "Vincent is paying her back for the time she signed the both of us up for a charity race last spring. And if she discovers she's been had, she'll up the stakes."

"If she finds out, your goose is cooked," Vincent said from behind the oriental screens. He popped his head around the corner and told them to come and eat right away or he'd throw their dinner to the sea gulls.

He didn't have to say it twice. Carlson and Cassandra shared a look that said "I dare you," then took Vincent at his word. Carlson calmly stepped over the coffee table and slipped between two armchairs as Cassandra ducked past an enormous elephant's ear plant and detoured around the back of the sofa. She picked up a pillow and tossed it in his direction, working on the assumption that he'd slow down to throw it back . . . and give her an edge in the race.

It almost worked. He threw it *and* hit her in the back of the head without breaking stride. They met in front of the oriental screens, Cassandra holding the lead until Carlson neatly crested a handy ottoman and pulled up beside her. Laughing, they scrambled for their chairs at the elegantly set table, nearly plowing over the reluctant chef in the process. A tie.

The chandelier swayed slightly, more a product of

the fast-moving air currents caused by their mad dash from the living room than any movement of the houseboat. A tinkling of its prisms was the only noise as Cassandra and Carlson shook out their napkins and proceeded to enjoy the first course.

Vincent stared at them from under thick, gray-tipped brows and shook his head. "You two used to have such nice manners."

Cassandra forked a bite of the Chinese chicken salad into her mouth and agreed. "You're supposed to take our eagerness as a compliment."

Vincent harrumphed and retreated to the kitchen as Carlson reached across the table to fill Cassandra's wineglass. "I would have beat you if you hadn't cheated."

"Who cheated?"

Carlson stared at the eyelashes batting furious innocence and darkened his expression. "The pillow," he intoned with a note of real threat in his voice. "You thought I wouldn't notice?"

She giggled. "Call it a handicap. I needed a momentary advantage." She was still laughing when the patently false reproach in Carlson's gaze turned to desire, then her laughter died as he explained to her, very softly, so that Vincent couldn't hear in the next room, the erotic merit of creative handicaps in lovemaking. . . .

Eight

"May I continue to rely on your discretion if I leave you to serve your own dessert?" Vincent asked after he'd set down the main course in front of them.

"I won't tell Mallory about the tennis thing," Carlson said with a lazy smile. "Although I can't speak for Cassandra."

Vincent shot her an assessing look that escalated to a threat when she smiled sweetly without saying a word. "You don't want to get mixed up in this war, Cassandra," he warned her.

"Marvelous dinner, Vincent," she said neutrally, aware that she was treading on thin ice. She didn't care, though. Being with Carlson the past two weeks had awakened in her a sense of adventure she'd never before experienced.

Being with Carlson made her feel alive.

"Yes, Vincent," Carlson said, "dinner is superb. We'll take care of dessert a bit later. What is it?"

"Apple crème brulée," Vincent said stiffly. "Considering the lack of notice you gave me, you're lucky it's not ice cream and cookies."

"I happen to like ice cream and cookies," Carlson mumbled.

Cassandra lifted her brows in question. "What time did you call him?" she asked Carlson.

"Around noon, I guess," he said offhandedly.

"More like half-past four," Vincent muttered. "And you wouldn't have gotten any dinner at all if Jake hadn't looked the other way when I was raiding the larder at the restaurant."

"Jake is too afraid of losing you to worry about a bit of petty theft," Carlson said. "In any case, I assume the bill for all this is already in the mail."

"Taped to the refrigerator," Vincent said, "although why you have three rolls of tape in the kitchen and not a single colander is a matter for a psychiatrist."

"You don't have a colander?" Cassandra asked, her brows raised in amazement.

"Mallory probably took it when she got married," Carlson fabricated. Actually, he wasn't entirely positive there had been one before she left the houseboat. Mallory wasn't any more interested in cooking than he was.

"I don't see how you get along without a colander," Cassandra said with frank disbelief. "I've got three."

Vincent looked as though he thought even three was inadequate, but didn't say so. He just told them there was decaf brewing in the kitchen and left them with instructions to eat before their dinners got cold. They heard the front door shut a short moment later.

"Vincent should have refused to cook at such short notice," Cassandra said.

"He cooks for dozens of people every night at the restaurant," Carlson said logically. "I can't see what difference it makes to do it over here."

Cassandra tried to remember that Carlson's familiarity with a kitchen began and ended with boiling water. She smiled and explained a few of the more significant problems Vincent might have encountered.

"Besides the fact that it isn't his kitchen and he has to look for everything he needs—some of which you obviously don't have—at the restaurant he has different people doing different jobs. One cook for sauces, another for breads, desserts. Busboys and waiters and a maitre d' to organize the service. He had to do it all by himself tonight."

"Keeps him on his toes," Carlson mumbled, and returned his attention to his salmon and pasta as instructed. After a moment, Cassandra followed his example.

Colanders! he thought, wincing. And that would be just the beginning of the changes Cassandra would wreak on his life if they gave any serious consideration to making their relationship a permanent thing. One day it would be colanders, and the next he'd be tripping over all the other gadgets that filled her much larger kitchen from top to bottom. Not to mention all that silver and crystal and china. And her clothes, of course. There probably weren't enough closets on the entire dock to handle that kind of volume.

And where the hell would they put the piano?

Carlson shook his head and took a sip of wine. By the time Cassandra moved her life onto the houseboat, there'd be nowhere left to breathe. And there would be the constant stream of people in and out, disrupting the even pace of his life.

He didn't want to change, particularly to adapt to a way of life that was totally abhorrent to him. No, Cassandra's life-style was unsuitable.

The woman, however, was very suitable. Too bad he couldn't have one without the other, he thought with a great deal of regret.

He pushed his empty plate aside and relaxed in his

chair as Cassandra finished her own dinner. "I'm sure," he said, getting back to her earlier comment about the lack of warning he'd given Vincent, "that if someone called you at the last minute to do a dinner, you'd be able to pull something together."

"Perhaps," she said.

"Don't be modest, Cassandra," he chided. "Mallory says your parties are models of perfect organization."

She fended off the compliment. "I thought you didn't approve of what I did for a living," she said over the rim of her wineglass, a smile beginning at the edges of her mouth.

"That was before I found out you were making a profit."

"And before then?"

"I thought you didn't have anything better to do."

Her smile faded, but Carlson didn't notice as he gave his attention to the task of refilling their wineglasses. A shiver of fear rippled up Cassandra's spine, and she would have run if there had been anywhere to go. But there wasn't. How could he know her so well, and not know that she really didn't have anything better to do? *She didn't even know how!*

"So as long as I'm making money, giving parties is a legitimate pastime?" she asked with forced lightness in her voice. She tried to keep her expression light as well, because he was getting close to the edge of the abyss that held all the fears and insecurities she didn't want him to discover.

Carlson cocked his head as he tried to identify the curious note in her voice, but her expression revealed nothing unusual. He proceeded with his makeshift apology.

"Don't be difficult, Cassandra. I'm trying to tell you that my digs at your career over the past months were unwarranted. You're good at it, you're making money, you're happy. The magic three." He didn't say that he liked her job any better than before, because that wasn't true. It also wasn't relevant.

"You're apologizing?" she asked, her mouth gaping open with the last bite of food hovering on her fork just inches from her lips.

He nodded. "I should have done it two weeks ago, I know, but we haven't exactly had any quiet time."

At last, she thought. An opening to distract him from talking about her work.

She grinned broadly. "You were awfully quiet last night after we made love on the dining room tab—"

"That wasn't quiet, that was exhausted!"

"That was *fun*," she teased, and lowered her voice seductively. She knew she was playing with fire and loved every second of it. "Dessert can wait, you know. Vincent will never find out from me."

"You're trying to change the subject." He growled something unrepeatable under his breath and rose to clear the table. Cassandra just giggled and let him do it. After her first taste of the Apple crème brulée, she said definitively that dessert couldn't wait after all.

Carlson ate his own dessert without noticing. His attention was on Cassandra, the woman he loved . . . and couldn't have.

The woman he loved. Realizing that hadn't brought him any joy, and he watched as she greedily spooned the rich dessert into her mouth.

She was strong and independent and forging a path for herself in a way of life that was totally foreign to his own. All the parties and dinners and entertaining were part and parcel of what she did, what she *was*. Take them away and she'd be left with nothing.

He'd asked her on the Wine Train if she would necessarily have to give up her profession if she remarried, and she'd answered of course. There would be no need to work, she'd said, no time with all the entertaining for her husband.

He couldn't offer her a life on her terms. His own was too different, too isolated. Parties were the exception, not the norm. Yet despite their disparate life-styles, he'd fallen in love with her.

Too bad, he berated himself. Loving her didn't take away the facts. He was no good for Cassandra.

She'd soon find that out. In the meantime, he had only one thing he could give her: herself. He'd made up his mind to teach Cassandra about who and what she really was. That was what loving was about after all, trying to do the best thing for the one you loved.

There was no place for him in her life, just as he'd once thought there was no place for her in his.

Without her entertaining, she'd have nothing of her own. And he could only offer her love.

It wasn't enough.

An affair, he'd promised her. Surely she'd know better than to imagine there could be more?

Cassandra finished her dessert in record time and looked a little surprised to see that Carlson had beaten her by a whisker.

"We were talking about your work," he said after pouring coffee.

"No, we weren't. We were talking about making love—"

"Work!" he interrupted. "And I'd be very happy if you'd keep your mind on it."

Cassandra sighed, then appeared reconciled and prepared to humor him. "You've already apologized very nicely and I accepted it. I don't really see what there is to talk about."

He shrugged and kept his tone casual. "Just curious, I suppose. We've never really talked about what you do."

"You're never 'just curious,'" she said with a speculative gleam in her eyes. "What gives?"

Carlson flashed what Mallory called his "smoothie smile," the one that was guaranteed to convince even the worse doubters. "You spend a lot of time doing whatever it is that you do, but even you admit that it's not like having a real job."

She smiled. "You have to realize that where I grew up, all the little girls were trained in the arts of entertaining. It's like keeping house, or driving. Everyone does it."

"How many of them make a business out of it?"

She laughed as though he'd said something funny. "What I do really isn't business, it's just a way of keeping busy."

"Your accountant thinks of it as a business," he pointed out, realizing this was going to be harder than he'd thought. Cassandra was stubborn in her belief that the thing she was best at—entertaining—wasn't a viable career. She was still looking at it as a stopgap between husbands.

"My accountant does that for tax purposes," she said. "According to him, if I make money, I'm in business."

"But you're really not."

"I'm really not." Finishing her coffee, she pushed the cup aside and folded her arms on the table. "You know and I know that I'm only doing the parties for friends, or friends of friends. They've learned that I'm available and it's convenient to let me do their entertaining. That's all."

"You don't advertise?"

"I have enough to do without that!" she said, and he thought her laugh was about as genuine as her determinedly bright expression. "Besides, I've only done this for people I know. I can't imagine strangers wanting to come for a party when they could just as easily go to a restaurant."

Carlson waited patiently for her to continue. She was afraid of something, and he would swear it was the same thing that frightened her every time they discussed her work.

All of a sudden, he realized what it was. He could have kicked himself for being so bloody stupid. *She was afraid it would go away.* She was afraid because she looked at all the parties and dinners as favors for friends, not a continuing enterprise.

She was afraid because she didn't have the confidence to see that she was better at what she did than almost anyone else out there.

He smiled. That was a second thing to teach Cassandra once he'd convinced her of her independent nature.

He'd teach her not to be afraid.

"Now show me yours."

Carlson slowly straightened from putting the last saucer into the dishwasher and leveled his gaze on the laughing woman perched on a stool. His not-shy, not-timid, and definitely not-reserved lover was teasing him once more, and he loved every moment of it.

He wanted it to last forever.

Cassandra laughed again as Carlson lifted a brow and said, "Excuse me?"

"I said 'show me yours.' We've spent dessert and washing up talking about my work." Her expression clearly meant to tell him that enough was enough. "I want to see where you do your thing."

Carlson threaded a dish towel through the handle on the refrigerator. "I presume we're talking about writing?"

"Of course!"

Taking the hand that he offered, she jumped down off the stool and followed him through the house and up a set of stairs. It was the first time he'd brought her to his home, and Cassandra was eager to see it all. It might be her only chance.

Sucking in her breath and flashing a covering smile at Carlson, she wondered at the rage that filled her every time she acknowledged her time with Carlson was a finite thing.

Rage, not sorrow.

Rage, not regret.

Rage. Not directed at Carlson, but at herself. And while she didn't understand the whys and hows, she was grateful. It kept her sane. It eclipsed the more fragile emotions that would have had her crumbling under the weight of a broken heart.

It gave her the strength to enjoy today and ignore tomorrow.

Carlson led her down a short hallway and into a small, dark room. It was plainly furnished with a desk, chair, and bookshelves. The computer took up most of the desk space, a stereo system a large part of the shelves.

"It's a bit dreary," she said with a grimace.

"No distractions," he said. "No window to look out, just me and the computer."

There was nothing wrong with his logic, she mused. But she'd had this image of Carlson sitting at a big desk in a decent-sized library—and of herself sharing the space with him. "I'd pictured you at one of those old typewriters, you know, the things with keys you can see and ribbons that need changing every few chapters." Her tone clearly indicated that any author worth his salt would live up to her imagination.

He laughed and drew her over to the desk. "The computer and I get along just fine. It's more flexible than a typewriter." He circled her shoulders with one arm and reached down to flip on the machine. It beeped and hummed, and when the screen stopped flashing, he selected a diskette from the drawer and inserted it. He tapped a couple of keys and showed her how the book looked on the screen.

"That's all you have to do?" she asked. "Turn it on and put in this little square thing?" Cassandra was a member of the disappearing faction of people who were still computer-illiterate.

"Diskette," he said automatically. "You've never used a computer?"

"Only once in college and it wasn't anything like this," she said, and sat down in the chair because she wanted to try it out. "That one was part of a bigger one—"

"Mainframe, probably," he interjected.

She shrugged. "Whatever. It was always overloaded and you practically had to get up in the middle of the night just to get some time on it. Unfortunately, at two o'clock in the morning, there wasn't anyone around to help me when it did something that I wasn't expecting, and I almost flunked the course before I finally figured out what was going on."

"I can teach you this machine in five minutes."

"Bet you can't," she challenged.

Carlson leaned over her shoulder and turned off the machine so that he could let her start it up herself. She did, twice, then selected another diskette to push into the disk drive. Carlson showed her how to open a file, then close and save it.

"And the rest is basically typing," he said. "This little scroll key over here lets you go from page to page, or you can use these arrows."

"That's all there is to it?"

"More or less. The word processing program needs

a little bit of study, but it's still basically typing. This particular program is user-friendly."

"You mean it won't blow up if I touch the wrong key?"

"It won't blow up," he confirmed with a grin. "And even if it did, I keep backup copies of everything important."

Cassandra glanced at the clock and noticed the lesson had taken ten minutes. "You lose the bet."

"So maybe you're a slow learner," he teased, and leaned past her to eject the diskette from the computer. He filed it away in the drawer and flicked the power off.

"Or perhaps you were thinking about something else?" she said to the blurred reflection of his face in the blank screen in front of her.

"Mm."

She twisted her head so that she could look up at him and discovered that his mouth was within kissing distance. It was a temptation, one that she had no trouble giving in to. Cassandra planted a flirt of a kiss on his lips and was pleasurably rewarded when he leaned down to prolong the contact.

As her mouth opened under the pressure of his, she felt his fingers in her hair, searching for the pins that held the chignon in place and drawing them out one by one. When they were all gone, he cupped the back of her head in his warm hand and held her still and hard under the assault of his mouth.

He kissed her as though he was ravenously hungry, and Cassandra responded in kind. It was the most natural thing in the world . . . to give passion to the man who unknowingly held her heart in his hands.

Much later, as she lay drained and exhausted in his arms, Cassandra again tasted the rage of her own inadequacy. She wasn't the woman he needed . . . the woman he could love.

•   •   •

Cassandra put down the telephone and stared vacantly out her kitchen window into the bright morning sunshine. She had, without a doubt, lost her mind. Then she looked at the notes on the pad on the counter and knew that she didn't have time to worry about it.

She had a party to give, that night, and only eight hours in which to prepare. She picked up the telephone and punched out Sonia's number.

"A dinner party for twenty-four, formal, cocktails at six-thirty," she told her assistant.

"I thought we didn't do last-minute parties," was Sonia's first printable comment.

"We don't, but this guy sounded so pathetic," Cassandra tried to explain. Sonia was right, and Cassandra was still trying to figure out why she'd let herself in for a mountain of work inside a molehill of a time frame.

"This guy?"

"James Brock," Cassandra said. "He's the president of some computer software company. Apparently, the restaurant where he was going to hold his party had a fire last night and somebody recommended us."

"Somebody? You don't even know who?"

"He gave me a name but I didn't recognize it. Probably someone who attended a party here." It had surprised Cassandra too. This was the first time she'd taken on a job that wasn't for someone she knew. The surprise was that it didn't bother her at all.

Her second-in-command pleaded for sanity. "I'm supposed to be apartment hunting today," Sonia reminded her. "My lease runs out here in less than a month and you know we're busy the rest of the week and most of the next!"

"Don't worry about it. You can have Peggy's room here until you sort things out."

"There are other restaurants," Sonia said.

"The man was absolutely frantic, Sonia. I just couldn't tell him no. He said something about overseas investors and how his job was on the line if he didn't come through with a spectacular dinner."

"You're soft in the head."

"That's supposed to be heart, Sonia."

"Both," the other woman said succinctly before asking for instructions.

Cassandra listed several people for Sonia to call before trying the chefs that might be available at such short notice. "If you can get Geoffrey to cook, we'll have lamb or beef. If it's Maurice, we'll do veal."

"What if I can't get either?"

"What's your specialty?"

Sonia groaned and hung up, leaving Cassandra to pray the worst wouldn't happen. It wasn't as though she and Sonia couldn't cook; they'd done it many times. It was just that they'd be busy enough getting things organized without having to do the cooking on top of everything else.

As it turned out, Geoffrey agreed but wouldn't be able to come until three, which meant Cassandra was still stuck with much of the prep work in the kitchen, as well as the shopping. She hung up the phone feeling only semigrateful for Geoffrey's compliance. Cutting vegetables was her least favorite chore. But there wasn't anything to be done about it, and ten minutes later she'd ordered the flowers and wine, both to be delivered midafternoon.

Then there was the grocery shopping to take care of, a deceptively simple-sounding process which entailed stops at three butchers, two vegetable markets, a bakery, and the supermarket. By the time Cassandra returned home, Sonia was directing the placement and setting of tables. The redheaded whirlwind tracked Cassandra back to the kitchen, giving nonstop updates of progress. They'd done a quick clean of the living room and the vacuum cleaner had sucked up part of a curtain, but they'd fixed it. The curtain would need minor surgery, however, time permitting.

Cassandra wrote it on the list of things to do that she kept near the telephone and refrained from asking which curtain. She didn't want to know. As long as it didn't show, it wasn't important.

Geoffrey called to tell them to put the lamb in a marinade, which Sonia then made according to his directions. Cassandra handed her the package of lamb cutlets and stuffed the vegetables into the refrigerator. There was a minor problem, Sonia reported as she tucked the cutlets side by side in the pan of marinade. One of the peach tablecloths had turned up with a grease stain and yes, she'd take care of returning it to the laundry tomorrow when there was time. She'd already put it on her list.

In the meantime, they were short one cloth and what color scheme did Cassandra want to use instead?

Cassandra didn't *want* to change colors at all because the flowers were meant to go with the peach cloths and now she'd have to call the florist again. It was Peggy's flower shop, and this time Cassandra spoke directly with her instead of the assistant she'd dealt with earlier. Peggy had obviously been talking with Mallory in the recent past and she asked broad, leading questions, like was Cassandra planning on coming to her wedding with Carlson and would they promise not to squabble in the middle of the ceremony? Cassandra said she didn't have time to chat but perhaps Peggy would like to call Carlson and ask him herself. After all, he was the one who started all their battles.

Peggy said she would do just that after she made the change in the flowers and hung up, leaving Cassandra to wonder if her quick tongue was going to get her into trouble sooner rather than later. She quit worrying the next second because the telephone rang and it was the frantic Mr. Brock again, and was there any way she could manage dinner for thirty instead of twenty-four?

No problem, she told him, and felt not even a prick of conscience as she added that the price tag would reflect a bit of fancy footwork. Then she yelled to Sonia to add another table and to use the off-white napkins and tablecloths on top of the mint green underskirts before letting herself out the back door for another trip to the butcher and baker. Thankfully, she'd bought enough vegetables the first time around.

She was really working up a sweat by the time she stepped in through the back door forty minutes later.

"Carlson called right after you left," Sonia said over the roar of the electric knife sharpener. "He's going sailing with friends this afternoon, and you're welcome to go along if you don't have anything better to do."

"Yeah, right!" she scoffed. "Carlson's under the impression that a dinner party is merely an exaggerated version of a picnic. He doesn't have a clue about how much work goes into this." Cassandra threw her purse onto a chair and popped the meat into the refrigerator.

"Does he even know you're working today?"

The light came on in her head and Carlson's invitation was no longer an absurdity. "You're right. I guess I forgot to tell him." Trying to shove aside the sense of impending senility, she laughed. "If it's not on my list, I don't do it. Did you tell him I was a little tied up?"

"Uh-huh." Sonia cautiously tested the knife on her finger and frowned as she put it back through the electric sharpener. She shouted over the metallic buzz of steel against the honing wheel. "He said he'd catch you later."

Later. Cassandra pulled an apron over her head and wondered if she'd make it until "later." But she knew she would, just as she knew she'd stay up half the night if Carlson was in the mood. As she snatched the razor-sharp knife from Sonia's hands and started to chop a handful of green onions, one of the girls came in from the other room to say there was a gentleman at the door who said he was a musician hired for tonight's party . . . and where could he set up the band?

At James Brock's insistence, Cassandra stood beside him at the door as he thanked everyone for coming and accepted their praise and compliments.

"A wonderful party, James," said a man that Cassandra recognized as a banker from Sausalito.

"Excellent idea, James. We need to do this more often." This from one of James's sailing buddies.

"Can't remember when I've had a better time," another buddy added.

James said he was glad they'd come. Again and again, as couples and singles walked past them and out the door, he smiled and said he was glad they'd all had a good time. Cassandra had met many of the guests before. Those that she hadn't, she'd spent part of the evening getting to know.

They were all from the local area, the greater Bay

Area if not Marin County itself. She'd noticed that little detail sometime during cocktails.

"The music was a wonderful touch, dear," a woman said to Cassandra. She added, "I've never seen a drummer on top of a piano, though. How did you manage that?"

"Just seemed like the place for him," Cassandra replied, smiling as she shook the woman's hand. Lack of choice was a more accurate answer, and she was anxious to check the finish on the baby grand underneath the thick layers of padding. It had been the only option, what with the sax and trumpet players standing in front of the piano. The drummer would have been in the middle of everything. It had been an inspiration, one that she didn't particularly like but then, what choice had she had? She had to admit, though, that because the lid on the piano was down, all the other musicians had had to mute their own playing. That had worked out very nicely, especially during dinner with only piano music in the background. And if the drummer was a little scrunched for space, well, it couldn't be helped.

Cassandra had told him firmly that he was not to fall off.

"Incredible meal, Cassandra," said Virginia White, the last guest to leave. On the far side of middle age, Virginia was extremely active in several local businesses and therefore a frequent guest in Cassandra's home. "But then," she added, "you always manage to do something spectacular, don't you?"

Cassandra smiled and walked Virginia to the stairs, to where her chauffeur was waiting. The older woman had had knee surgery the previous spring, and while she was managing nicely now, steps were not to be taken lightly. Returning to the front door, Cassandra found James Brock beaming at her from the hallway.

She had a bone to pick with him. A big one. She led him into the living room and over to the bar where she poured herself a glass of wine. He helped himself to a soda, and she waited until he'd turned back to her, still smiling brightly.

"Foreign investors?" she said quietly.

"Oops." The smile faded to be replaced by a look of such total chagrin, she almost laughed.

She didn't, though. She was entirely too angry for that. And tired. Anger predominated, though, and she made sure that the expression on her face accurately reflected her feelings.

James Brock was in big trouble.

Nine

I. J. Carlson was in big trouble.

Cassandra fumed as she picked up empty coffee cups and carried them into the kitchen. There were no foreign investors.

Her anger simmered as she pulled the layers of padding off the piano, then carefully folded and put them away. There had been no restaurant fire.

She seethed as she replaced the unused glasses in the cabinet and tidied the bar area. James Brock's job hadn't been on the line.

James Brock owned the computer software company and didn't answer to *anyone*.

All that was left was the washing up, and Cassandra made a command decision to let Sonia and a single dishwasher manage without her. The breakage rate would be lower that way, she rationalized.

"Leave the crystal for tomorrow," she told them. "I'll do it in the morning. It'll be late enough by the time you finish the rest and we've all had a hard day."

"Good decision, boss," Sonia said, and began to gather the fragile glasses onto a tray.

Cassandra checked her watch and figured they'd

put in better than a twelve-hour day. Nonstop. Her temper on boil, she grabbed her purse and snapped her bill up from the counter.

"Why didn't you give that to Mr. Brock?" Sonia asked, eyeing Cassandra warily.

Cassandra kept her tone even because she didn't want to frighten either of the women with the ferocity of her anger. She wanted to save it all for Carlson. "Because Mr. Brock didn't throw the party. A Mr. Carlson did."

"Our Carlson? That nice writer you're dating?"

Cassandra nodded. "One and the same. Our Carlson. Soon to be known as 'Black-eyed Carlson.'" Cassandra experimented making a fist and couldn't remember if the thumb went inside or out. No matter, she decided. She'd ask Carlson; he was the expert.

"Why?" Sonia asked.

"Because I'm going to punch his lights out," she stated with a huge measure of satisfaction.

Sonia gulped and looked as though she believed her. "No, that part's easy to figure out. I meant, why did he do it?"

Cassandra didn't really know the answer to that, not yet, but it was logical to assume he'd reverted to his old tricks. "Because he wanted to make me crazy. Remember the time he screwed a red light bulb into the fixture on the front porch?"

"I thought that was kids!"

"It was that no-good rat Carlson. He admitted it the other night," she said, grinding her teeth because it had been funny just a few days ago. When he'd confessed to that prank, she'd thought they'd quit playing those games.

"This was all a practical joke?" Sonia sounded as though she wanted to do a little punching herself.

"Looks like it," Cassandra said. "I'm on my way to

find out." She rushed down the hall to the front door, en route to her car. She normally kept it in the garage, but it was now parked at the curb. One of the waiters had borrowed it to pick up extra ice buckets—for the champagne James Brock had brought without warning—and he'd found the driveway blocked when he returned.

"Take no prisoners!" Sonia shouted after her.

Cassandra slammed the door behind her and marched down the stairs, muttering obscenities that would have shocked her if she'd paid attention to what she was saying. She didn't, though, just like she wasn't paying attention to where she was going. Head bowed, shoulders squared for battle, she charged down the front walk and plowed straight into the target of her wrath.

"Hi."

Cassandra rocked back and would have fallen were it not for Carlson's hands on her arms. "You!" She shook off his hands and took a step back to give herself room to swing.

He caught her fist single-handed, which was a good thing because she dropped her purse and swung the other fist. He caught that one too.

"Stop that!" he said, straightening his arms to keep her flailing fists away from his face. "You'll break your thumb if you hit me with it tucked inside your fingers."

That answered that question. Cassandra glared at him and pulled her thumbs out. "Let me go so I can do this right," she demanded.

"You can't brawl on your front lawn," he said reasonably. "What will the neighbors think?"

"Blow the neighbors!"

"Cassandra, your language! Why don't we take this inside?"

"Because I don't want to break anything besides

your face!" She tried pulling and punching, but Carlson held onto her wrists and easily directed her flailing movements away from his head. "Let . . . me . . . go!"

"Simmer down, Cassandra," he said, and she was infuriated by the hint of a grin tugging at his lips. "You can punch me after I explain."

"Explain what?" she asked hotly. "How amusing it is to watch me work 'til I drop?"

"There's a reason behind it."

"*Reason?*" she shouted, finally succeeding in freeing her wrists. She didn't attempt another hit, though, choosing instead a tactical retreat of two steps. She'd tell him what she thought of him first, then she'd work on that black eye. "The only reason I can figure out is that you're an ignorant writer who gets his kicks playing tricks on people!"

"Trick is a bit harsh," he said mildly, shoving his hands into his pockets when it appeared he didn't need them for his immediate defense. "It was more of an exercise."

"*Exercise!*" Cassandra grabbed her purse from the ground and thrust her arm through the shoulder strap—another weapon, she calculated—then dug through the contents until she found the bill for the night's party. "This *exercise* just cost you your next advance!" She held the bill in front of his nose until he plucked it from her fingers.

Carlson's gaze dropped to the bottom line and he admitted that she wasn't all that far off. It appeared that Cassandra was going to take financial as well as physical revenge. He grinned—a silly thing to do, considering it infuriated her even more. "I heard it was a great party."

She eyed him incredulously. "Did you actually think I wouldn't find out it was your idea?"

He thought it was interesting that her voice had

softened to a deadly calm. "To be honest, I had hoped to tell you myself. I didn't count on James's goof with the foreign investor bit. That wasn't in the script at all. He ad-libbed, I guess, and forgot about it the moment you agreed to do the party."

"*Script!*" She stomped her feet in frustration, but quit when the heels of her pumps began to wobble. This was getting weirder by the minute, but it didn't faze her. She had a little ad-libbing of her own she wanted to try out on him. "You know, Carlson, I've never asked you what your initials stand for. I. J. Carlson. Now I wonder . . ."

He cleared his throat to tell her, but she was too quick for him.

"I've got one. How about 'I'm a Jerk' Carlson?" She frowned and shook her head. "No, that's too easy." She pretended to think about it for a second, then snapped her fingers. "I know. 'Insufferable Jackass' Carlson."

"Cassandra—"

"Oh, drat! That won't work either. Jackass and Carlson are redundant."

"Irwin James," he said dryly, and waited for a new volley of insults.

"*Irwin James?*" She felt the laughter build in her chest and had absolutely no compunctions about letting it out. "Irwin James?" she repeated through the giggles. "No wonder you never tell anyone."

"There's nothing wrong with my name," he said, but without much hope that that would stop her. He'd taken flack all his life for the "Irwin" half of his Christian name, and doubted that Cassandra would come up with anything original.

"I don't know," she said with a malicious smirk. "I think Irwin goes rather well with Jackass. We still have the redundancy problem with Jackass and Carlson, though."

"That's enough, Cassandra," he said firmly. "I came over here to talk to you about the party, not to play name-calling games."

"Oh, yes, the party," she said, all amusement wiped from her expression. "The reason I worked myself silly, all day, while you were out sailing with friends."

He sighed heavily and tried again. "I made up this party for you. To prove something to you."

"*What?*" She was all out of insults anyway, so she stared up at him with anger in her expression and the first twinge of curiosity in her thoughts. What possible reason could he give for making her work her butt into the ground?

"To prove that you could do it," he said. "That you're good, that it isn't just one of those nice little useless accomplishments you learned at your mother's knee—"

"I never said—"

He held up his hand to hush her. "Just because you never had any formal training, or because it's not much different from what you feel is a wife's job, you think it doesn't have value. You feel like you're dependent on your friends for business when it's all you can do to keep up with everything they ask of you. You said it yourself, you don't advertise because you don't have time for more business."

He hadn't done it for a lark, she suddenly realized, but she was too dazed to tell him she'd just figured that out.

"It's a real job with real responsibilities," he went on, "and it takes knowledge and experience to do it well."

She stared at him.

"If you never got married again, you could do this for the rest of your life and be *successful* at it."

Her mouth dropped open.

"Cassandra Lockland," he said with stern formality, "you are an extremely independent, self-reliant woman who doesn't need anyone to lean on." Since she no longer looked so ready to throw a punch, Carlson took a chance and closed the distance between them. He put his hands on her shoulders and squeezed reassuringly.

"No one?" she asked in a small voice.

"No one. And if all your friends moved to Alaska tomorrow, you'd just have to advertise a little and you'd end up with the same thing: A business that is healthy and prosperous."

"You're insane," she breathed.

"Nope. I'm right and I won't give up until you admit it."

"Why?"

"Why the dinner party? I just explained that. Shock tactics. I wanted you to do the impossible just to prove you could."

"No." She raised her hands and placed them on top of his. Her palms absorbed his warmth as her mind absorbed his intent. "I understand the party, but I want to know something else." She took a deep breath, looked into the eyes of the man who'd come to mean everything to her, and asked the one thing she truly didn't understand. "Why did you bother at all?"

"Because I love you."

Cassandra couldn't have predicted his answer because it was the last thing she'd ever imagined him saying. Her fingers curled around his, and she knew her nails were digging into his hands, but she couldn't do anything about it. Physical responses were totally out of her control.

His dark eyes held her stunned gaze and she found herself asking him to say it again.

"I love you, Cassandra," Carlson slipped his arms around her shoulders, bringing her close so that she couldn't see the overwhelming regret he couldn't hide. Tonight was the only time she'd hear him say those words. Tonight was their last night together.

He'd decided that earlier, when he'd realized that every day he spent with Cassandra, he loved her a little more. Another day, and he was very much afraid he wouldn't be able to let her go.

But he wanted one more night.

"I want what's best for you," he said slowly, rocking her against his chest and feeling enormous relief when she slipped her arms around his waist. "I couldn't stand by and let you go through life thinking you were less than you are."

"So you had to show me," she whispered.

"Well, you certainly wouldn't listen. I tried that."

The night was probably cold, Cassandra thought idly as she snuggled against Carlson under the light of an old-fashioned iron street lamp. The neighbors might have been drawn to their windows by her screeching too, and were still watching.

She didn't care.

"Carlson?"

"Hm?"

"Do you love me because I'm independent and strong and not shy?"

"So you admit you're not the clinging vine you've always believed?"

"Maybe. I'm working on it." Bursts of revelation were coming too quickly for her to assimilate them all, and she was more interested in the love part than the dependency thing. "Answer my question first. Are you in love with me because you think I'm not clingy and all those other things you hate?"

"No. I fell in love before I figured that part out." Unable to stand there any longer without reliving the experience of kissing her, he tilted up her chin with one finger and took her lips.

It was like the first kiss of a new day . . . a new

beginning. Cassandra's heart swelled with joy and love, and she lifted herself to his mouth because she wanted more. Carlson gave all that she asked and demanded she surrender everything in return. Their mouths danced and mated, and they would never have stopped if a passing car hadn't honked its approval.

"You did it for me," she said softly, staying within the circle of his arms until he drew her firmly to his side and began the short walk back to her house.

"For you," he said. Certainly not for himself, he thought. If he'd been just a little more selfish, he might not have done it at all. By opening her eyes to herself, he'd destroyed any chance they had for happiness.

Of course, it was all a figment of his imagination, all these visions of what could have been if only he hadn't been so damned noble and unselfish. He wasn't really ruining anything because he'd admitted his love for her—and she hadn't said anything in return.

What had he expected? he asked himself. A spontaneous "I love you" just because he'd said the words?

And what the hell did it matter? Tomorrow it would all be over between them, and he could at least walk away knowing he hadn't broken her heart. Still, he couldn't help but wish she cared enough to miss him when he was gone.

"You made me go to all that trouble because you love me," she murmured when they reached her porch.

"Because I love you." As he said the words again, Carlson knew he'd never say them to another woman in his lifetime.

Cassandra loved him so much in that moment, she almost told him. She didn't, though, because she wanted to make it special.

Later, she promised him silently. She would tell him, using the words she'd never dreamed he would want to hear from her, and then she would show him. But first . . .

She gave a pathetic moan that demanded his sympathy. "I worked really hard. So did Sonia and the rest of the crew."

"I know," he said resignedly. He'd have to make his apologies in those quarters another time.

"My feet hurt."

"I'll rub them."

"Sonia was supposed to go apartment hunting today and she's going to be homeless if she doesn't find something." Cassandra forgave herself the slight exaggeration.

"I'll help her," Carlson said, wondering if Sonia was going to react as belligerently as Cassandra had about his little exercise. He hoped not.

"The vacuum cleaner ate a curtain," she continued.

"My fault?" he asked, lifting an eyebrow in doubt as he pushed open the door and pulled her inside.

"Of course." Cassandra threw her purse on a table where it landed with a thud. A formidable weapon indeed, she mused, and laughed at her recent aggression. Anger? No, that must have been someone else. The only thing she felt was absolute joy. "If things hadn't been so rushed this afternoon, the person vacuuming would have been more careful."

"What else?" he asked, not really wanting to know. Between the exorbitant tab and his dubious complicity in the case of the ruined curtain, this was costing a sight more than he'd expected. He consoled himself with the sure knowledge that at least he'd gotten off without a black eye.

"Just one thing." She led him through the now-quiet house to the kitchen. There was no one left, and she guessed they must have departed via the back door—deterred, no doubt, by all the activity out front. Nearly all signs of the day's frantic activity had been swept, cleaned, and polished away.

All except the crystal.

Pointing to the dozens of fragile goblets clustered beside the sink, she smiled and gave him the bad news. "Hand wash and dry, if you don't mind."

"Me?"

"You."

"Tonight?"

She nodded.

"Cassandra?" he asked with dry amusement.

"Hm?"

"Is this revenge?"

"No." Crossing the kitchen, she opened a drawer and pulled out a stack of clean towels. "Revenge is a bit harsh. I prefer to think of it as an *exercise*."

Cassandra stepped out of the bath and dried herself slowly, lingering over the process because she had all the time in the world. Carlson wouldn't be done with washing the crystal for ages.

Her skin was warm and soft from the bath, and the faint scent of lavender followed her as she walked into the dressing room. The sexy nightgown that Carlson had bought her was draped over the back of a chair. She slipped it on over her head and smoothed its nearly transparent length down her body. Turning, her bare toes curling into the thick pile carpet, she stared at her reflection in the full-length oval mirror.

She didn't look any different than she had the night Carlson had given her the exotic nightgown, she mused. That surprised her, because everything had changed. There should have been some physical sign of her enlightenment, but her searching gaze found nothing out of the ordinary. Eyes, nose, mouth—they all looked the same. Her hair was piled on top of her head in a loose knot with damp tendrils clinging to her neck, slightly disorderly but almost identical to how she always put it up for a bath.

How could one's life change so radically and leave nothing tangible to mark the phenomenon? A mystery to be sure, she decided, and flicked off the light as she went into the bedroom.

The lights from beside the bed threw deep shadows across the room, too dramatic for her mood. Cassandra rummaged in a chest and found some candles. She placed them on the small table between the chairs near the windows and lit them. The softening effect of the candlelight made all the difference. She left the bedside lights on, too, because they'd discovered they both preferred making love that way, in the light.

She smiled and snuggled deeply into the cushions of one of the chairs, tucking her feet under her as she waited for the bedroom door to open. Making love with Carlson was about to take on a whole new meaning.

She'd gone from shy to bold just a couple of weeks ago, not so much a conversion as an acknowledgment. And tonight, Carlson had succeeded in convincing her that she was a very independent and capable woman.

Cassandra didn't doubt his assurances. It made so much sense when she put it all together. Coming from a background that had nurtured dependent females, she hadn't recognized her own strengths. She hadn't known what to look for.

She laughed softly and marveled that she'd been too dense to figure it all out for herself years ago. What an idiot! All that time spent worrying about what would happen if the parties disappeared. It had never occurred to her that her entertaining career was a product of her own considerable talents and not simply dependent upon the generosity of friends and acquaintances.

It was really a business, she thought with a surge of pride, and not something she did because she didn't know how to do anything else.

Now that she understood that she was in control of her future, she was no longer afraid. Carlson had given her that. As surely as he'd exposed her true nature, he'd given her the ability to believe in herself.

Because he loved her.

Five minutes later, Carlson opened the bedroom door without knocking and found Cassandra curled up in one of the chairs. She was beautiful, and he knew it had nothing to do with the candlelight. Her hair caught the flickering light and glistened like molten gold, and he decided that the first thing he would do was loosen the knot that held her hair up and run his fingers through its silky length.

And then he'd—

"Carlson?"

"Hm?" The gown, he decided after a bit of thought, would stay. For a while. It would drive her mad when he teased her with the fragile barrier between them.

"Are you coming in?"

He shut the door and leaned against it as he contemplated the taste of her. "I'm not sure," he drawled. "I've never had dishpan hands before."

"And you think I'll mind?"

"Only one way to find out." He took his time crossing the room, enjoying the changing definition of her barely clothed body as the candles flickered in the cool draft from a slightly opened window. One moment he could make out the curve of her breast, and a second later the budding nipple was distinctly visible beneath the sheer gown. Another step and he cut across the light from the bedside tables, and his shadow slashed over her upper body, leaving only her legs discernible.

And her feet.

Cassandra pulled her legs out from under her with the intention of rising to meet him, but that wasn't what he had in mind.

"Stay there, love," he murmured, and in the next moment he was sitting cross-legged on the floor in front of her chair. "I remember you complaining about sore feet?"

She giggled. Having Carlson pay close attention to her feet hadn't been at the top of her list of what she'd expected when he walked in the door. "That was a lifetime ago," she said with a hint of speculation in her voice. "You could probably bribe me into forgetting your promise to rub them."

"I could," he agreed as he took one foot into his hands and started to massage it. "But I think the possibilities here are interesting enough."

"Um." Cassandra was won over in five seconds flat. Stretching out her leg so that he could more comfortably hold her foot near his lap, she propped the other one on his knee and dropped her head back against the cushions.

His hands were magic, but she already knew that. Still, it was an agreeable surprise to discover that his talents extended to include those parts of her body that weren't particularly sexy. She moaned as he molded and squeezed and petted, thoroughly involved in the pleasure of her first-ever foot massage.

"You like?"

"I like," she breathed, then yelped a few moments later when he squeezed her foot sideways and she heard muted cracking noises. Her head came off the back of the chair as she tried to retrieve her foot from his grasp. "Rub, don't break!"

"A little therapeutic popping never hurt anyone," he said with a laugh, and rubbed a little harder. "Your feet are tense."

"So would yours be after six hours on three-inch heels," she muttered, reluctantly resuming her relaxed pose. The "therapeutic popping" had felt good, she admitted, but she wasn't sure she was ready for more of the same.

His fingers delved between her toes, rotating each digit one by one until even they, too, were relaxed. Cassandra went back to moaning every now and again, her gaze lazily following the dancing shadows on the ceiling. He changed feet, setting the now-limp one gently in his lap before taking the other into his warm hands.

Cassandra had never felt so pampered in her life.

"Carlson?"

"Hm?"

"I love you."

Carlson's hands stilled for a millisecond as the words he'd most dreaded hearing left her lips. Then he resumed the massage, denying her sentiment with a joke. "You're just saying that so I won't stop rubbing your feet."

"There's that," she granted, laughing a little when he ran a finger up the sole of her foot. "You are very good at this."

"I come from a long line of feet-rubbers. My mom used to tell me she only married my dad because he was so good at it."

"It's probably an inherited skill. But that's not why I said it. I love you and I knew it before you started rubbing."

There it was again. Carlson wished she wouldn't, because it would make everything so damned hard tomorrow. He couldn't speak, not even to tell her she didn't know what she was talking about.

"I just thought I'd tell you now," she added, "before the evening progressed any further." Her eyelids drifted shut as his fingers took to stroking the bottom of her foot in a steady cadence.

"You thought you might forget to tell me?" It would have been better that way, he thought.

"No, silly." She groaned as his fingers dug into the ball of her foot. "But I didn't want to tell you when we were making love. It seemed a little tacky to me, shouting it out for the very first time in the middle of passion. Kind of like saying 'thank you,' you know? And besides, there's so much going on anyway when we're making love that I was afraid it might get lost in the shuffle. I didn't want you to miss it."

Carlson couldn't stop the chuckle, even though the last thing he felt like doing was laughing. "What about afterwards?" he asked. He should drop it, he told himself, but he was fascinated with her unique viewpoint on the subject of when one should or shouldn't make her first declaration of love.

"Afterwards, I'm usually asleep," she said dryly. "You should know that by now."

He started on her toes, concentrating on what he was doing and trying to come up with a way to keep her from saying anything more, anything she would regret when he was no longer with her. But he couldn't think straight, not when the woman he loved was trying to give him the most wonderful present he'd ever had—her love. He sighed, and hated himself for not being the man who deserved to take it.

The massage was having a soporific effect on her. While the conversation should have been riveting, Cassandra was so at peace, she couldn't help but let the rhythm of his hands lull her into a state of almost unconscious relaxation.

He loved her. She loved him. They were right for each other. They had been all along.

Carlson had taken away the barriers that forced them apart. Together *forever* was now a reality, not a dream.

Ten

She was going to sleep on him.

Carlson tickled the sole of her foot, but her toes just curled over his fingers. He tried another round of therapeutic popping, yet the cracking noise failed to elicit more than a moan of contentment.

Having Cassandra fall asleep on him wasn't how he'd intended to begin their last night together.

Carefully, so as not to disturb her—not that he really thought it was a possibility—he lifted her feet from his lap and rested them on the floor. After pulling off his shoes and socks, he stood up to strip off his clothes. He piled everything in the other chair before returning to his place at her feet. His body was rock hard with desire, and he wondered if she'd mind if he pulled her down onto his lap without any warning at all.

He wanted to do it, was all set to test the readiness between her legs with his fingers, when she stretched her arms into the air, then dropped them across the back of the chair, elbows pointing to the ceiling. Her small breasts thrust against the gown and he saw that her nipples were soft.

Cassandra wasn't ready. She wasn't even on the same wavelength, he realized with a muffled laugh. The foot massage had totally succeeded in relaxing her.

He could wait, he decided—not that he had a lot of choice in the matter.

His hands resumed a slow massage of one foot, and he heard a soft sigh from above. He was gentle with her, but firm. No cracking or popping to alter her state of semiconsciousness, but enough pressure to keep her from falling totally asleep.

She stretched her leg out and he had to lean back so that her toes wouldn't encounter his bare chest. He wanted her unsuspecting, unprepared.

He watched her face in the flickering candlelight and knew he'd never forget the sense of absolute peace he saw there. He smiled to himself because that expression would soon change to one of passion and he had a front-row seat. Laying the one foot aside, he took up the other and repeated his deceptively innocent massage.

"Carlson?" she murmured without opening her eyes.

"Yes, love?"

"Can you keep that up forever?"

He stifled a laugh as his gaze dropped to his straining arousal. "It would be an interesting challenge," he said mildly, and decided it was time to change the pace.

He gathered the hem of her gown up around her knees then ran his hands along her calves and resumed the massage.

"That's nice," she sighed, and wiggled her butt deeper into the cushions. If Carlson was amenable to the idea, she rather thought she'd let him do this every night.

Carlson ignored her lack of response as his fingers

worked the tight calf muscles for what he felt was an adequate period before moving to her knees. His fingers grazed the tender area behind them, and she giggled. She didn't resist when he casually pushed her knees several inches apart.

Then, without any warning, he splayed his fingers across the soft skin of her thighs and waited.

Cassandra went from an idle acceptance of his touch to an instantaneous awareness that it had changed. His hands were hot and firm on her thighs, not moving yet holding her legs apart with a steady pressure that was erotically exciting. Her breathing cruised full speed from deep and sure to shallow and erratic, matching the wild thumping of her heart. She opened her eyes so that she could look at the man who'd brought her from near-sleep with such easy mastery.

What she saw brought a gasp of surprise from her. "You're naked!" she exclaimed as she stared at his hard arousal and wondered how she could not have known.

"You mind?" he asked pleasantly, and pushed her gown to her hips so that he could see her as his hands continued their skillful massage.

"I missed it."

"You haven't missed anything, Silk," he murmured, and told her to lie back and relax. "I've only just gotten started."

"I can't relax," she protested. She started to lower her arms to her sides, but he told her to leave them where they were. She complied because he told her if she didn't, he would stop.

"But I want to hold you," she said, her head falling back as his fingers skated across her belly, then returned to her thighs without stopping anywhere vital.

"You will," Carlson assured her, fascinated by the

ease with which he could make the muscles of her tummy clench by simply touching her. The gown was bunched at her waist now, her swollen nipples pushing against the soft fabric and tempting his mouth.

He waited, though, content that she was no longer unaware of his intentions, and practiced the fine art of teasing without touching those places where she most wanted his caress.

Cassandra moaned and tossed her head back and forth, willing him to put her out of her misery yet wishing it would never end. He teased and taunted, and when he finally slipped his fingers across the damp heat between her legs, she nearly bolted out of the chair.

It was all a blur after that. Cassandra tried at one point to pull the gown over her head. Carlson resisted her efforts, murmuring something about textures and variations, and she quit trying because his mouth was suddenly hot on her breast and she understood.

They were in the chair, together, and she really didn't know how that was possible. She was aware of Carlson's thighs tight around hers and an absence of breath as his mouth took hers in a dramatic joining that hushed her cries. Then there was the rough brush of carpet on her breasts as she lay flat on her tummy with Carlson straddled across her hips, continuing his massage on her back. But she didn't want her back rubbed, she told him, and he laughed and varied the pattern of his strokes until she was squirming beneath him. When he finally pulled the nightgown over her head, she was beyond caring.

She saw rockets and stars and then more stars as he sent her past the edge of any resistance again and again, soothing her with bargains of "soon" and "next time" when she tried to take him with her.

But it wasn't soon, she knew. She was half-exhausted and winded and slick with her sweat and his before he lifted her from the floor and carried her to the bed. The sheets were cool and smooth at her back, though, as far as she was concerned it could have been a bed of nails. The only thing she responded to was Carlson's touch, the feel of his arms around her, his lips hard against hers.

Dragging him down with her, she used her hands and lips and teeth to bring him to the verge of insanity, just as he'd done to her. She could only take him to the edge and no further, though. She couldn't send him spinning off through the stars alone because he refused to go without her. He wouldn't let her push him past that point, not this time, he told her.

"But you did it to me!" she screamed in abandoned frustration as he pushed apart her legs and entered her with a single thrust.

He lay on top of her without moving, gathering his energy, his strength, then used a precious part of it in praise. "You're so incredible, Silk. All soft and open and giving me everything that you have without a single thought to holding back." He lifted himself onto his elbows to look down at her, because he wanted her to know he fully recognized the gift of her love. Threading his fingers into the damp tendrils of hair at her temples, he held her misty gaze with his own. "I love you so very much."

She grinned. "That didn't sound tacky at all," she said softly.

"I need you to know I mean it," he said, not smiling at her little joke. He was too involved in absorbing every little detail about her. Her cheeks were flushed and shiny with sweat, and the scent of lavender mingled with her sweet breath. She looked up at him with trust and love, and he knew that she believed him.

He wanted her to have that much to hang onto, because tomorrow, when he faced her with the unchangeable facts and walked away from her forever, he hoped she'd remember that he hadn't left because he didn't love her.

Cassandra wrapped her legs around his hips and drew his face closer to hers. He was so serious, she mused, and she was a bit miffed that he wouldn't let her have her way. He'd engineered for her a succession of sensual highs without taking anything for himself, and she wanted to be the one in control, the one to send him hurtling over the edge. "I wanted to give you—"

"Hush, love," he whispered against her lips. "I know you did. And maybe later, if you're awake. We'll see."

"If you weren't stronger than me, I'd have won." She clenched some critical muscles around the hard steel of his manhood in retribution.

"You're stronger than you think, Silk," he said, and thrust his tongue deep inside her mouth. There he began a rhythm that matched another, taking his cue from Cassandra and accelerating from slow to mindless when she wordlessly begged him to hurry.

This time he went with her to that magical place of bright lights and pure sensation . . . holding tightly in his arms the woman who would never leave his heart.

It was dawn when he left her, asleep in her bed and oblivious to his parting. The note he'd spent an hour composing wasn't the best example of his literary skills, but it didn't matter. It was the message that counted.

He went into the bathroom and propped the folded white paper against her toothbrush holder. She'd find it there, probably after her shower. Her eyes wouldn't be open much before then.

Stealing one last glance at the softly snoring woman only partly visible in the confusion of pillows and blankets, he said a soundless good-bye and left the room. Treading softly, he went downstairs and let himself out the front door.

The engine in his car turned over with a minimum of fuss and noise. He pulled away from the curb and accelerated quickly down the street before the overwhelming surge of second thoughts could send him running back into the house and into her arms.

He was ending their affair. Now, before it became an impossible thing to do. Now, before he lost the thin edge of reason that kept him from taking what he wanted and to hell with what was best for her.

He hadn't meant to leave her with only a note, but it had occurred to him as she lay sleeping atop his chest that it was really his only choice. Had he tried to explain why it was over, she would have argued. Cassandra never believed anything he said until he proved it to her, and this was something even he couldn't show her.

Writing it down in black and white was his best shot at convincing her.

Carlson turned left and pulled onto the freeway on-ramp with as much enthusiasm for the drive home as he had for eating pansies.

Her hand shook and the note fell from her fingers. Cassandra swore and picked it up again before it was soaked by one of the puddles of water on the floor. She tossed the note onto the vanity, then carefully knotted the towel above her breasts until she was sure it wouldn't fall. When she'd wrapped another towel around her head, she snatched up the crumpled piece of paper and marched into the bedroom and over to the window. She pulled open the drapes and in the uncompromising light of another spectacular Bay Area morning, she reread Carlson's words:

> Cassandra,
>
> Until I discovered those little secrets you were keeping from everyone, including yourself, I thought you were merely a beautiful woman—too weak, too clingy, too dependent for me. Definitely not the woman I needed in my life.
>
> I am now faced with the knowledge that I am not the man for you . . . although I would give my soul if things could be different. They can't, though. I'll never be able to accommodate myself to your way of life—the parties and all that goes with them. And I can't expect you to forsake for me those things that make you what you are.
>
> You're strong and independent and will someday find a man who leads the kind of life that will nourish your strengths.
>
> I regret that I am not that man.

She curled her fingers around the note, crushing it in her fist. It was all she had left of Carlson, just a few words on a piece of paper.

She threw it into the wastebasket.

Pulling the towel from her head, Cassandra strode back into the bathroom and began the routine of getting ready for the day. She dried her hair, set it in hot rollers, and applied a light cream to her face as she waited for the curls to set.

She wondered if he'd thought she would cry. Fat

chance, she fumed, too furious with him to give in to tears.

The rollers came out and Cassandra brushed her hair until it lay soft and gleaming around her shoulders. When that was done, she stared blankly at her reflection and wished she knew what to do next.

String him up by his thumbs, perhaps. Or boil him in oil.

It was a toss-up.

She applied mascara, blush, and lipstick. Other methods of barbaric torture flitted through her mind as she left the bathroom and confronted the tangle of sheets and blankets that pretty much eclipsed the shape of the bed.

Her gaze was caught by the nightgown he'd pulled from her body just hours ago, a bit of lace and silk and not sexy at all to look at—not as it was now, crumpled and half-hidden beneath a chair. Her feet took her across the room although her conscious mind hadn't given the instruction. She knelt on the floor beside the discarded gown and wondered if it had all been a dream.

I love you so very much, he'd said. She'd believed him because it was the thing she most wanted in the world, Carlson's love.

She still believed him. A piece of paper couldn't change that.

Cassandra clutched the gown to her heart and knew what she had to do. No tears, she mused, and finally understood. She hadn't cried because it wasn't over.

Carlson just thought it was.

Rising to her feet, she dashed into the dressing room with the gown in one hand, tearing off the towel around her with the other. She slipped the wrinkled gown over her head, ignoring her reflection because it didn't matter how she looked.

She'd get her point across however she was dressed.

Cassandra smiled for the first time since finding Carlson's note of good-bye. Everything was going to be okay. She knew it. Still, butterflies fluttered in her stomach as she pulled a full-length beige coat of raw silk from its hanger and put it on over the nightgown.

All the independence in the world didn't matter if Carlson wasn't around to enjoy it with her.

Cassandra heard the sound of his footsteps coming toward her and said a silent prayer of thanks that he was home. She said another prayer when he opened the door.

Then she threw the note in his face. The crumpled piece of paper ricocheted back at her. She caught it and threw it at him again. This time her aim was less precise and it sailed over his shoulder.

"You left something," she snarled, and pushed her way past him before he could stop her. Getting inside was critical. He might have said, "Thank you, but I have nothing more to say," and closed the door in her face.

He didn't—or she didn't give him the chance—and she tramped down the hall to the living room. She walked straight to the bar and rummaged in the small refrigerator until she found a can of soda. Breakfast, she warned her stomach as she flipped open the top and took a long gulp. She was on her second swallow when she caught sight of Carlson. He'd followed her into the living room and was half sitting on the back of a chair, his feet crossed at the ankle and his gaze trained on her.

He didn't look at all happy to see her.

"Where are your shoes, Cassandra?" he asked, his voice even and low and distant.

Her toes curled into the carpet, and for a split second she felt as if she'd been transported back in time, to the days when he'd taken such pleasure in teasing her with her shortcomings. It was only a brief regression to her former self. She'd come there to knock some sense into him, not to twitch under his microscope.

The last thing she was going to admit was that she hadn't even realized she was barefoot.

She returned his gaze with confidence and strength, all the time squashing the fear that threatened to topple her. "Remember the Cassandra prophecy?" she asked softly, determined to keep things civil, if she could.

Of course, if he'd simply paid attention and accepted what she said, there would be no reason to shout. She didn't want to yell at him, but she would if she had to.

She'd do anything to keep him from ruining their lives.

He nodded in answer to her question. Unable to stand the totally dispassionate look in his eyes, she turned away from the bar and wandered over to the fireplace. "She predicted things that people didn't believe, but she was never wrong."

"I remember," he said, a note of impatience in his voice.

She faced him again, hurrying on to what she needed to say before he threw her out or just left himself. "I predict," she said clearly and slowly, "that if you don't forget all that nonsense you wrote and come back to me, on a permanent basis, you will be miserable the rest of your life."

"Tell me something I don't know."

It wasn't the answer she'd expected.

"Then what the hell is this all about?" There, she'd yelled. She felt better now. Shoving her hands into her pockets of her coat, she steeled herself for his counterpunch.

"I explained it in the note—"

"You didn't even sign it!"

"I figured you'd know who it was from." Carlson abandoned his deliberately indifferent pose and walked toward her. It would be easier if he stayed away . . . but he was totally incapable of doing that. "I put it in writing so you'd understand."

"I wouldn't understand if you lectured me on the subject from now until next Christmas," she shot back. "You finally convince me I'm independent and strong and I'm beginning to get the idea that I could *possibly* be the kind of woman you might fancy sharing a few years or so with . . . you even go as far as to tell me that *you love me* . . . and then you say sorry, it still doesn't work for me?"

"That's not what I said." Carlson clenched his jaw and tried to keep his hands to himself. Touching her was out of the question.

He couldn't think straight if he did that.

"I said that it won't work for you. I can't give you the kind of life you need."

Hope, Cassandra thought. She had figured that was what the note had meant, but she hadn't wanted to believe it until she heard the words from his lips.

Perfect.

"Why?" she asked, her eyes wide and innocent as though she didn't understand.

"You know why." Taking a couple of deep breaths, Carlson went over the rationale in his mind, then repeated it word for word aloud. "You are successful and happy at what you do, giving parties. If you stay with me, I can't give you that. For one thing, the houseboat isn't big enough to accommodate anything more than a small gathering."

He raked his fingers through his hair, and Cassandra noted with immense pleasure that he didn't look as well-groomed as usual. Perhaps, he wasn't quite in control.

"For God's sake, Cassandra, I don't even *like* parties." He turned away and strode over to the bay window, keeping his back to her as he continued his diatribe. "I'm an *author*, not a corporate executive. I don't *need* your kind of support in my life."

He'd taken the bait, and Cassandra started to reel him in.

"All you've done since the first time you kissed me is manipulate me and make all the bloody decisions about how *I'm* supposed to live my life, about what *I* need to be happy, and you know what? I'm getting a little fed up with it!"

She waited a couple of beats for him to jump into the argument. He didn't, though, and fear would have won if she hadn't already decided to put everything on the line—her pride right up there with her love for this incredibly stubborn man.

"Irwin James Carlson," she said in a voice loud enough to get his attention, "you are an arrogant, macho jerk and if I didn't love you so much, I'd walk out right now."

He turned, but she couldn't tell if he was interested or merely acknowledging the level of frustration in her voice.

"I should have said Insufferable Jackass Carlson," she corrected herself, not worrying about being interrupted. He was looking surprised that she was pursuing the matter when he'd thought it was settled. "I've given it a lot of thought and can't seem to get around the Jackass part. It fits."

He shrugged.

She smiled. She took one step toward him, then another when he didn't shy away from her approach. Before she spoke again she was standing nose to chest with him, her head tilted back so that she could see his chin.

It would have been nice if she could see his face, but she settled for the unshaved chin.

"Did you ever," she asked softly, "for one moment, imagine that I might not *want* to live with you here?"

He granted her silent wish and bowed his head. They made eye contact. "The houseboat?"

She nodded.

"I just assumed—"

"Just like you assumed that I would throw away everything I'd worked for and come be your bride," she said. "No wonder you didn't think it would work. You didn't *think*!"

"You don't want to marry—"

"Not that, Jackass!" she said with all the exasperation of the last hour fully evident in her tone. "I do want to marry you."

Carlson gaped at her. "Then you want to keep working?" He felt like slamming his fist into his face. She'd told him otherwise, and it had never occurred to him that she might change her mind.

She nodded. "I certainly can't imagine keeping busy supporting any kind of a social life you'd generate. One party a year isn't much of a challenge."

He shook his head in confusion. "But you told me—"

"When?" she asked quickly.

"Two weeks ago, when we were in Napa. You said you'd quit if you remarried."

She kept her expression impassive. "A couple of things have changed since then, in case you didn't notice. Or did you think I'd discover this dynamic independent woman inside of me only to throw her away when I got married again?"

He looked poleaxed.

She could almost taste success, and she didn't give him a chance to recover. "About what you said about living on the houseboat, Carlson. Why did you assume we would have to live here?"

"Because I work here," he said as if it were the most logical answer in the world. "I don't want to give it up."

"You'd rather give me up," she said flatly, because that was exactly what he had done. She almost cried out from the strain of waiting for him to make some kind of answer, but didn't. He was standing too close, and any show of weakness might lessen her bargaining position.

"No," he said.

Victory. She smiled for the first time since she'd come into his home.

"So which is it, Carlson? Do you want me or your houseboat?"

"I have to choose?"

He didn't wait for her reply, preferring instead to put his hands on her hips and haul her against his body, where he knew she would feel his heart slamming against his chest. He took her mouth with a fierce possession that told her without words that the matter was settled.

The tears finally came, filling her eyes and rolling down her cheeks. She didn't suppose she would have noticed were it not for the salty flavor his kiss assumed. Laughing and crying at the same time, she wiped her eyes with her fist and told him it was all his fault. "Promise me you won't ever write another note like that again," she said.

"What note?" he murmured against her lips, then

his tongue stroked away her tears as she lifted her arms, locking her hands behind his head.

"Carlson?"

"Hm?"

"I love you."

He smiled and nibbled a path from the corner of her eye to the tip of her nose, taking his time before he said the words he'd never thought he'd share with her again. "I love you so very, very much, Cassandra," he said softly, and dusted her cheeks with his mustache. He wanted her to laugh, not cry. "Although how you can love an arrogant, macho jerk is quite beyond me."

She giggled, just as he'd intended. "Hard to believe, isn't it? But I guess as long as you're *my* arrogant, macho jerk, I can put up with you."

He told her she didn't have a choice, because he never intended to let her go.

She belonged to him, just as he belonged to her.

To hell with the houseboat.

He sought the sweet, welcoming warmth of her mouth and showed her with his kisses that he meant what he said.

Forever.

End of discussion.

Eleven

Not quite.

Cassandra tore her mouth from his and fled to relative safety behind the sofa. Her fingers clutched the thick cushion and she didn't know if her stomach was clenching and curling because of the upcoming negotiations or if it was because of the gleam in his eyes.

He looked as though he was about to make love to her right there on the sofa and she wasn't entirely opposed to the idea.

They had business to settle, she reminded herself, and wondered what he'd do when he discovered what she was wearing under her coat.

"What are you doing over there?" he asked.

"We have a few points left to discuss," she said steadily. "Don't move!" she warned him when he started to round the corner of the sofa. "I want to get through this."

"I sell the houseboat, we move into your place, and I try to write amid the chaos of all the parties. What's left to discuss?" He smiled as she edged backward in an attempt to keep some distance between them.

"You're doing it again!" she exclaimed. She feinted to the right before diving over the sofa landing on her feet in front of the fireplace. She grabbed a heavy brass poker from the hearth and held it out menacingly when he advanced on her. "You're making decisions and I want you to stop it! And stay back!"

Carlson let her have her way, but not because he couldn't have wrestled the poker from her with little or no effort. She knew that, just as she knew he'd decided to go along with her despite her pretense at being in charge.

She glared at him and he grinned back, retreating to the sofa where he sat down and waited for her to speak. Dropping the poker from its attack position, she began. "This isn't going to work if you don't understand one very important thing."

"What's that, love?" He thought she looked magnificent, her eyes sparkling with fury and determination underneath that gorgeous white-gold mane. How had he ever imagined she would go peaceably out of his life? he wondered, and thanked heaven that she hadn't.

"I'm a strong, independent woman—"

"Agreed."

"Be quiet and listen," she admonished, but couldn't help the smile that curved her lips. "I'll start again." She took a deep breath. "I'm a strong and independent woman who is perfectly capable of participating in any decision-making process, particularly when any such decision involves me." Her gaze dared him to disagree.

He didn't, so she continued. "Keeping that in mind, I've got a few suggestions that merit our joint consideration. Here's the first one."

"I'm ready," he slipped in, just to let her know he was with her.

"We keep both the houseboat and my home," she

said, and ignored the expression of complete surprise on his face. "I know it's not the most financially sound thing to do, but I can't see that we have anything to worry about. As long as I want to continue working, I'll need a place to do it. The same goes for you."

A curious arrangement, Carlson thought. He mulled it over for a minute before asking a crucial question. "When I told you earlier that I would never let you go, it was in my thoughts that we'd be spending all our nights together."

"Of course," she said.

"So won't having two households make living together a bit complicated?"

"Probably."

"Where do you plan on us living, Cassandra?" he asked a little impatiently. Living out of suitcases wasn't the way he'd imagined spending the rest of his life, but if it made her happy . . .

She frowned. "I really don't know. Your closets are too small, but there are always masses of people traipsing in and out of my place. I think I'd prefer a bit more privacy than that."

He grinned. "Let me know when you decide."

She nodded, then said, "You're going to have to change your attitude about my parties."

"I already have," he said, wiping the smile from his face because he wanted her to know he was serious. "It occurred to me that I don't object to the parties themselves as much as I object to your spending so much time away from me. I was jealous."

"And now you're not?" she asked quietly.

"No, I'm still jealous, but I spend some pretty strange hours writing myself. I guess I was looking at it a little too subjectively." He let out a deep sigh and finished. "I respect what you do for a living."

"Thank you," Cassandra whispered, and she knew then that it would work.

"Anything else?" he asked after a long silence.

She looked up in surprise, then remembered the big number three on the list of decisions she'd formulated on the drive over. That had been optimistic thinking, making a list, because she'd had no guarantee she would get as far as convincing him he'd been wrong.

She smiled. "I think we should get married."

"When?"

"Soon." She put down the brass poker because it was no longer required. Carlson was proving more malleable than she'd imagined.

He nodded in agreement without making a single move to take advantage of her lack of defenses. Cassandra added one more point to her list. It appeared that if she didn't take the initiative, he'd go on sitting there, by himself, for ever.

"I think now might be a good time to kiss me," she said with a hint of demand in her tone. She didn't want him to think it was an option.

"You're sure about that?"

"Yes. If you think you can be bothered."

He leered, and she knew he was bothered all right. "If you're staying, you could probably take off your coat."

"Are you trying to tell me what to do again?" she asked slyly.

His instant frown told her he was going to put his foot down and remove her coat for her if she gave him an argument, so she slipped the buttons free and pulled the coat open.

Carlson's breath caught in his throat as Cassandra shrugged the coat from her shoulders. Stunned, he watched her walk toward him, the rays of the morning's brilliant sun streaking straight through the flimsy nightgown to reveal her every curve and secret.

He grinned and decided that maybe Cassandra wouldn't mind if he decided to make love to her without consulting her for her opinion.

First, though, his mouth touched hers in a caress that was unmistakably a kiss. After all, she'd proposed he do it, and he had learned the hard way not to ignore the suggestions of the strong, independent woman he so passionately loved.

Carlson checked that his seat belt was securely fastened, because the way Cassandra steered her little car through the narrow streets was enough to make anyone take precautions. She drove much like Mallory—a lot of zip and pizzazz and hard on the nerves until you realized she was actually very good.

Carlson did realize it, but he couldn't help if his reactions were on the defensive side. He *hated* being in the passenger seat.

He'd rather not be in the car at all, but Cassandra had—*finally*—remembered her day's busy schedule and she'd insisted he come along to help. "It's time you learned the nuts and bolts of entertaining," she'd told him as she'd hustled him down the dock to the parking lot.

"Nuts" pretty much said it all as far as he was concerned, but he'd held his tongue in as much the same manner as he was trying to do now, what with Cassandra ignoring speed bumps and yellow lights.

"I've got an idea about the closet problem," she said, halting her mad gallop out of Sausalito to allow a dog to cross the road. "What about changing that extra bedroom next to yours into a dressing room and closet?" Dog safely on the curb, Cassandra resumed her cruising speed in three seconds flat.

"That's an idea," he agreed, his mind only half on

what she said. The other half was wondering if her driving was substantially different with shoes than without. He'd argued against letting her drive at all, but Cassandra had still been in the "I want to make my own decisions" frame of mind and he hadn't stood a chance.

"If we decide to live at your place, though," she went on, "that will leave mine empty." She chewed on her bottom lip as she considered the problem and maneuvered the sports car toward the on-ramp of the northbound freeway.

"You wouldn't mind living at the houseboat?"

"No. I like it." Accelerating to merge into the swiftly moving traffic, she shot him a grin. "Not to mention that living on the houseboat will keep you out of my hair during parties."

"A reasonable goal," he drawled, and casually braced his hand against the dashboard, just in case Cassandra put off acknowledging the slowing traffic ahead.

She downshifted smoothly and lobbed a disdainful sneer at his precaution. "We still have the problem of my house," she said, her foot firmly hitting the brake as a mauve hatchback tucked into the gap between her car and a pickup truck. "Leaving it empty every night is asking for trouble. Besides, the zoning laws and such might not let me operate a business from a residence that is otherwise unoccupied."

"What if someone else lived in the house?" he asked.

"Such as?"

Carlson cleared his throat, wishing he didn't have to touch on a subject better left for another time— like ten years from now when she finally forgave him for throwing that last-minute party in her lap. "What about Sonia? You mentioned she was having trouble finding a place to live."

Cassandra grinned. "That's the first good suggestion you've made all day."

"Seems to me that making love was my idea," he murmured, and leaned over to drop a kiss on her cheek.

"I just let you think that." She laughed and patted his thigh before returning her hand to the gearshift. Traffic picked up a little, and within minutes she was able to slip into the right lane and exit into Mill Valley. Whistling her enjoyment of the day and the drive and, not to be forgotten, the man in the bucket seat beside her, she made a couple of quick turns and was soon moving at a good clip along the curving road that led to her home.

Ex-home, she corrected herself. The houseboat, complete with Carlson, was home now.

"You think Sonia will agree?" he asked.

"Absolutely. I can keep a little for rent out of her check, but nothing like what she was paying before. And she'll have the run of the house." Cassandra thought about it some more and asked Carlson what he thought about offering a partnership to Sonia one day soon. "She works as hard as I do. And if business keeps booming like it has, I'll want someone to assume a lot more of the responsibility."

"So that maybe you can spare some time for your poor, browbeaten husband?"

She steered into her driveway and parked the car at the back door. Turning in her seat, she smiled up at him impishly. "Maybe. And maybe I'll just want a little extra time to catch up on my reading."

Carlson snaked an arm around her waist and dragged her over the console, a maneuver that wouldn't have been possible if Cassandra had been less petite . . . or less willing. In between nibbling at her throat and ears and tickling a couple of places, he gave her a few reading suggestions of his own, beginning with page eighty-four of *The Seventh Kiss*.

It was after eleven that night before they made their way back to the houseboat, and long past twelve when Carlson promised Cassandra that if she'd just give him a short break to recuperate, he'd show her something new.

She laughed and said, "You couldn't if you wanted to."

He muttered something about independent women being too sassy for their own good and pulled a blanket over their slowly cooling bodies.

"Forty winks," he promised over a wide yawn, and shut his eyes. "You worked me too hard today, woman. I need to rest." He wondered if all her days were as frantically busy as that day had been. If they were, he couldn't understand why she wanted to work at all.

"But I'm not sleepy," she protested, running a finger across his mustache and giggling when he tried to stop her by snapping at her with his teeth.

"Yes, you are," he said. "You're always sleepy after sex."

"'Always' just isn't the case tonight. I'm too excited to sleep."

"About what's going to happen when I wake up?" he teased. He turned her body so that her back was nestled against his chest and her hands didn't have the opportunity for exploration.

"I have to admit to a certain amount of curiosity," she said, "but it's getting married that's got me wide awake."

"Scared?"

She shook her head and snuggled closer under his

chin. "Impatient. I want to get it over with before you come up with a better idea."

"I won't be coming up with anything if you don't let me get some sleep," he cautioned, tightening his forearm around her stomach to show her he meant business.

There was silence for approximately ten seconds before she spoke again. "Carlson?"

"Yes, Cassandra?"

"Do you have anything to read?"

He groaned . . . then was hit by the perfect solution. "What would you think about reading the new book?"

"But it's not done yet," she said, startled that he would even make the suggestion. An unfinished novel seemed so private, so intimately personal.

"True, but I wouldn't mind if you wanted to have a look at it." Carlson was surprised himself to realize he very much wanted Cassandra to read what he'd already written, the first four chapters of Book Three, Untitled.

He wanted to know if she liked it.

"You're sure you don't mind?" she asked.

"Positive."

She was thrilled.

Cassandra slipped out of bed and sorted through his closet until she found a shirt that would keep her warm in the cool autumn night. As she buttoned it and rolled up the sleeves, Carlson reviewed the computer procedures and told her, between yawns, in which drawer the diskette was filed. She figured he was asleep before she left the room.

Feeling like she was on the threshold of a new adventure, Cassandra quietly pulled the office door closed behind her, flipped on the desk light, and settled herself in front of the computer.

She turned it on. It worked. Delighted that she'd

achieved that much success, she pulled open the drawer and began flipping through the dozens of diskettes she found there, searching for one labeled "Book Three, Untitled."

She found it easily and was lifting it from the drawer, when the label of the diskette immediately behind it caught her eye: The Cassandra File.

"What on earth . . ." she murmured, pulling it out so that she could get a better look at it. "The Cassandra File," she read again, and wondered if it could possibly be the title of another project he was working on, a new book he hadn't yet shared with her.

A novel he'd named for her. Cassandra thought she rather liked that idea.

She gently inserted the diskette into the opening of the computer as Carlson had taught her, then waited as the machine made the appropriate whirs and beeps.

Curiosity killed the cat, she reminded herself, then grinned because she didn't feel the least bit of guilt at delving into this mystery she'd stumbled upon.

He wouldn't have sent her into the computer room at all if there was something he didn't want her to see, she reasoned, and hit the keys that were supposed to bring the text up on the screen.

She was so pleased when the computer cooperated, it took her a few moments to settle down and read. Once she finally got started, though, a bomb wouldn't have distracted her.

Her breath hissed between her teeth as she slowly realized it was not a book in the making, but a painstakingly explicit recounting of her affair with Carlson.

From his point of view.

She was outraged that he would put it all in writing, but even so, she could not drag her eyes away from the screen. She scrolled down, page by page, intent upon not missing a single word.

She rediscovered every intimate detail of her affair with Carlson.

It was shockingly riveting.

She blushed when she read how he'd reacted to her striptease in the kitchen, and surprisingly felt a wave of pleasure wash over her as he described thoroughly the immense satisfaction he'd enjoyed at her sensual aggression.

Why had he written it down?

Her blush turned to flames as he described the night he'd given her the nightgown, the glimpses of her almost naked body an enticement he'd found impossible to resist.

She wondered if maybe she ought to kill him for putting into words their private encounters.

He even admitted his exhaustion the night they'd made wild, uninhibited love in the dining room, accurately interpreting Cassandra's passionate response to his demanding caresses.

It was a breach of privacy.

Toward the end, he wrote long passages about how much he loved her.

There was nothing from the last twenty-four hours, but he hadn't had the opportunity, she realized. He'd been with her—loving her, leaving her, and loving her again.

It was that realization that brought it all into perspective.

With a calculating gleam in her eyes, she scrolled back to the beginning and carefully reread all the intimate, sensual details.

The Cassandra File was dynamite.

It was a work of love.

"Ready when you are," he suddenly said behind her.

Cassandra clutched at the keyboard in fright before her nerves settled enough to transmit the message that it was only Carlson.

Only Carlson. She smiled grimly. Time for a little surprise of her own. She summoned her initial reactions in support of a round of gentle admonishment.

"I really think you ought to have told me, Carlson," she said smoothly, scrolling back to the encounter in the kitchen without turning around. "The Cassandra File is fascinating. I didn't realize how much you enjoyed that little striptease last week."

Silence.

"But then, it appears you liked the dining room just as much." She scooted the chair closer to the screen and searched for the appropriate page. "Here it is: *Her fingers laced with mine, and I took advantage of this to push her arms above her head. Her hair spilled like a golden pond on the gleaming mahogany. I looked down at her, her mouth swollen from our kissing, and began to torment her with my—*"

"I can explain," he interrupted.

"I think you've already done that quite nicely," she replied, and scrolled forward a couple of pages. "Especially here when we were—"

"You're angry."

"Angry doesn't begin to describe my feelings," she said in a deliberately emotionless voice, thinking a more appropriate word might be "aroused."

"I didn't mean for you to see that."

"I already figured that out for myself," she said, scanning the text as she looked for something appropriate with which to tease him. He deserved a little teasing.

Apparently, he couldn't think of anything to say, and Cassandra decided she was much too excited by her discovery to chastise him any further. This would be much more fun if they could share it, she thought. Whirling the chair to face him, she allowed her gaze to drift over his casually naked body. She had to fight herself to keep from running straight to him.

He looked thoroughly miserable, though, and that was not how she wanted him to feel at all. She hurried to reassure him with the same honesty he'd shown in his writing. "I'd only be angry, Carlson, if you kept this from me forever."

His expression raced from miserable to stunned. "You don't mind?"

She blushed. "I have to admit I was a little taken aback, when I first started reading." She slid out of the chair and crossed the narrow gap between them to rest her hands on his shoulders. "But once I found the part about how much you love me—"

"It's true," he said urgently, cupping her face in his hands. "I love you more than I'd ever dreamed it was possible to love someone."

"I know that." She rose up on her toes to touch her lips to his chin, then his mouth when he dipped his head. "And I guess I'll just have to get used to my every move being recorded for posterity."

"That's not what I intended," he said against her lips, his fingers moving to the buttons of her shirt so that they could share the warmth of their bodies. He was beginning to shiver in the night's cool air. "It started out as being some sort of inspiration—"

"Sex helps you write?" she laughed, and gloried in the strength of his arms as he swept the shirt from her shoulders and drew her up against him, her mouth again within reaching distance of his.

"You help me write," he rephrased it, and planted a hot, wet kiss on her lips. "Once I got over that writer's block—"

"Thanks to me?"

"Thanks to you," he granted, his hands wandering down her back to her bottom, then pulling her closer. "As I was saying, once I got over the writer's block, I found I could write whenever I wanted. I did all of chapter four yesterday."

"Yesterday?" She pushed back a couple of inches and thought about it. "Yesterday, you invited me to go sailing, and I couldn't because I had to work."

"I invited you because I *knew* you had to work." He made a mockery of her attempts to shy away as he held her tightly in the circle of his arms. "If the truth were known, I probably worked as hard as you did."

"I doubt it. Sitting at a computer can't be as tough as you think it is."

He swatted her fanny. "Just try writing a book someday and maybe then you'll understand tough."

"I'm busy enough, thank you," she said, then kissed his chest and asked very politely if he would carry her back to bed.

"You ready for that 'something new' I promised you?" he asked, swinging her up in his arms after reaching over to flip off the computer.

She grinned and tickled his mustache with the top of her tongue. "Actually, I wouldn't mind trying page six of The Cassandra File, now that I know how much you like it."

Carlson asked her to describe it, in detail.

From her point of view.

She did.

THE EDITOR'S CORNER

As summer draws to a close, the nights get colder, and what better way could there be to warm up than by reading these fabulous LOVESWEPTs we have in store for you next month.

Joan Elliott Pickart leads the list with THE DEVIL IN STONE, LOVESWEPT #492, a powerful story of a love that flourishes despite difficult circumstances. When Robert Stone charges into Winter Holt's craft shop, he's a warrior on the warpath, out to expose a con artist. But he quickly realizes Winter is as honest as the day is long, and as beautiful as the desert sunrise. He longs to kiss away the sadness in her eyes, but she's vowed never to give her heart to another man—especially one who runs his life by a schedule and believes that love can be planned. It takes a lot of thrilling persuasion before Robert can convince Winter that their very different lives can be bridged. This is a romance to be cherished.

Humorous and emotional, playful and poignant, HEART OF DIXIE, LOVESWEPT #493, is another winner from Tami Hoag. Who can resist Jake Gannon, with his well-muscled body and blue eyes a girl can drown in? Dixie La Fontaine sure tries as she tows his overheated car to Mare's Nest, South Carolina. A perfect man like him would want a perfect woman, and that certainly isn't Dixie. But Jake knows a special lady when he sees one, and he's in hot pursuit of her down-home charm and all-delicious curves. If only he can share the secret of why he came to her town in the first place . . . A little mystery, a touch of Southern magic, and a lot of white-hot passion—who could ask for anything more?

A handsome devil of a rancher will send you swooning in THE LADY AND THE COWBOY, LOVESWEPT #494, by Charlotte Hughes. Dillon McKenzie is rugged, rowdy, and none too pleased that Abel Pratt's will divided his ranch equally between Dillon and a lady preacher! He doesn't want any goody-two-shoes telling him what to do, even one whose skin is silk and whose eyes light up the dark places in his heart. Rachael Caitland is determined to make the best of things, but the rough-and-tumble cowboy makes her yearn to risk caring for a man who's all wrong for her. Once Dillon tastes Rachael's fire, he'll move heaven and earth to make her break her rules. Give yourself a treat, and don't miss this compelling romance.

In SCANDALOUS, LOVESWEPT #495, Patricia Burroughs creates an unforgettable couple in the delectably brazen Paisley Vandermeir and the very respectable but oh so sexy Christopher Quincy Maitland. Born to a family constantly in the scandal sheets, Paisley is determined to commit one indiscretion and retire from notoriety. But when she throws herself at Chris, who belongs to another, she's shocked to find him a willing partner. Chris has a wild streak that's subdued by a comfortable engagement, but the intoxicating Paisley tempts him to break free. To claim her for his own, he'll brave trouble and reap its sweet reward. An utterly delightful book that will leave you smiling and looking for the next Patricia Burroughs LOVESWEPT.

Olivia Rupprecht pulls out all the stops in her next book, BEHIND CLOSED DOORS, LOVESWEPT #496, a potent love story that throbs with long-denied desire. When widower Myles Wellington learns that his sister-in-law, Faith, is carrying his child, he insists that she move into his house. Because she's loved him for so long and has been so alone, Faith has secretly agreed to help her sister with the gift of a child to Myles. How can she live with the one man who's forbidden to her, yet how can she resist grabbing at the chance to be with the only man whose touch sets her soul on fire? Myles wants this child, but he soon discovers he wants Faith even more. Together they struggle to break free of the past and exult in a passionate union. . . . Another fiery romance from Olivia.

Suzanne Forster concludes the month with a tale of smoldering sensuality, PRIVATE DANCER, LOVESWEPT #497. Sam Nichols is a tornado of sexual virility, and Bev Brewster has plenty of reservations about joining forces with him to hunt a con man on a cruise ship. Still, the job must be done, and Bev is professional enough to keep her distance from the deliciously dangerous Sam. But close quarters and steamy nights spark an inferno of ecstasy. Before long Sam's set her aflame with tantalizing caresses and thrilling kisses. But his dark anguish shadows the fierce pleasure they share. Once the chase is over and the criminal caught, will Sam's secret pain drive them apart forever?

Do remember to look for our FANFARE novels next month—four provocative and memorable stories with vastly different settings and times. First is GENUINE LIES by bestselling author Nora Roberts, a dazzling novel of Hollywood glamour, seductive secrets, and truth that can kill. MIRACLE by bestselling LOVESWEPT author Deborah Smith is an unforgettable story of love and the collision of worlds, from a shanty in the Georgia hills to a television studio in L.A. With warm, humorous, passionate characters, MIR-ACLE weaves a spell in which love may be improbable but never impossible. Award-winning author Susan Johnson joins the FAN-FARE list with her steamiest historical romance yet, FORBIDDEN. And don't miss bestselling LOVESWEPT author Judy Gill's BAD BILLY CULVER, a fabulous tale of sexual awakening, scandal, lies, and a passion that can't be denied.

We want to wish the best of luck to Carolyn Nichols, Publisher of LOVESWEPT. After nine eminently successful years, Carolyn has decided to leave publishing to embark on a new venture to help create jobs for the homeless. Carolyn joined Bantam Books in the spring of 1982 to create a line of contemporary romances. LOVESWEPT was launched to instant acclaim in May of 1983, and is now beloved by millions of fans worldwide. Numerous authors, now well-known and well-loved by loyal readers, have Carolyn to thank for daring to break the time-honored rules of romance writing, and for helping to usher in a vital new era of women's fiction.

For all of us here at LOVESWEPT, working with Carolyn has been an ever-stimulating experience. She has brought to her job a vitality and creativity that has spread throughout the staff and, we hope, will remain in the years to come. Carolyn is a consummate editor, a selfless, passionate, and unpretentious humanitarian, a loving mother, and our dear, dear friend. Though we will miss her deeply, we applaud her decision to turn her unmatchable drive toward helping those in need. We on the LOVESWEPT staff—Nita Taublib, Publishing Associate; Beth de Guzman, Editor; Susann Brailey, Consulting Editor; Elizabeth Barrett, Consulting Editor; and Tom Kleh, Assistant to the Publisher of Loveswept—vow to continue to bring you the best stories of consistently high quality that make each one a "keeper" in the best LOVESWEPT tradition.

Happy reading!

With every good wish,

Nita Taublib

Nita Taublib
Publishing Associate
LOVESWEPT/FANFARE
Bantam Books
New York, NY 10103

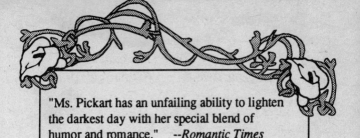

"Ms. Pickart has an unfailing ability to lighten the darkest day with her special blend of humor and romance."   *--Romantic Times*

THE BONNIE BLUE
by Joan Elliott Pickart

Slade Ironbow was big, dark, and dangerous, a man any woman would want — and the one rancher Becca Colten found impossible to resist!

Nobody could tame the rugged half-Apache with the devil's eyes, but when honor and a secret promise brought him to the Bonnie Blue ranch as her new foreman, Becca couldn't send him away. She needed his help to keep from losing her ranch to the man she suspected had murdered her father, but stubborn pride made her fight the mysterious loner whose body left her breathless and whose touch made her burn with needs she'd never understood.

"an overwhelming love story.... engrossing....Excellent!"
—*Rendezvous*

*He was every woman's dream lover
... and one woman's passionate destiny*

The
Matchmaker

by *KAY HOOPER*
author of STAR-CROSSED LOVERS

His name was Cyrus Fortune -- and he was as
enigmatic and elusive as the mysterious forces that
brought him to Richmond. He was secretly desired
by a score of women and openly envied by dozens of
men, but only the ravishing Julia Drummond ignited
his restless soul. She was the beguiling society
beauty who had never known the thrill of true
passion. Powerfully drawn to him she would defy
convention and scandalize society by breaking her
most sacred vows.

"For all of the fans of Ms. Hooper's "Once Upon a Time"
Loveswepts ... a uniquely exciting and satisfying
prequel.... Enjoy! Enjoy! Enjoy!" — *Heartland Critiques*